KEEPING THE BARREL OF THE GUN POINTED DEFEN-
sively at the man's motionless body, she tiptoed
toward him.

"Wake up," she suggested firmly, only half-
hoping that he would. An unconscious creep would
be much simpler to deal with than one who was
fully awake. With any luck, she could just roll his
sleeping body right back out the door.

Only, Cat wasn't sure she could budge him by
herself. The man looked just too big for her to try
to maneuver alone.

"Wake *up*," she insisted again.

The man still didn't move.

Cat leaned a little closer. His broad back was
still moving steadily up and down in a slow, rhythmic motion. His breathing was just fine, thank you.
It was his hearing that needed help.

Cat turned her gun toward the ceiling. What
difference would a little bullet hole make up there,
anyway? The plaster was already crumbling away
in great, gaping clumps. No one would even notice
the mark, but with any luck, the stranger would
certainly notice the noise. Being careful to aim
clear of the chandelier, she pointed at a stray spot
of paint and fired.

The stranger groaned. His eyes flashed open,
turning toward Catalina in vague comprehension.
"What the devil? . . ."

"My question exactly," Cat finished for him,
leveling the gun again squarely at his head. "What
the hell are you doing in my house, mister?"

WHAT ARE *LOVESWEPT* ROMANCES?

They are stories of true romance and touching emotion. We believe those two very important ingredients are constants in our highly sensual and very believable stories in the LOVE-SWEPT line. Our goal is to give you, the reader, stories of consistently high quality that may sometimes make you laugh, sometimes make you cry, but are always fresh and creative and contain many delightful surprises within their pages.

Most romance fans read an enormous number of books. Those they truly love, they keep. Others may be traded with friends and soon forgotten. We hope that each LOVESWEPT romance will be a treasure—a "keeper." We will always try to publish

LOVE STORIES YOU'LL NEVER FORGET
BY AUTHORS YOU'LL ALWAYS REMEMBER

The Editors

Loveswept ®
868

YOUR PLACE OR MINE?

CYNTHIA POWELL

BANTAM BOOKS
NEW YORK · TORONTO · LONDON · SYDNEY · AUCKLAND

YOUR PLACE OR MINE?
A Bantam Book / January 1998

ISBN 0-553-44589-8

Published simultaneously in the United States and Canada

Bantam Books are published by Bantam Books, a division of Bantam Dou-
bleday Dell Publishing Group, Inc. Its trademark, consisting of the words
"Bantam Books" and the portrayal of a rooster, is Registered in U.S.
Patent and Trademark Office and in other countries. Marca Registrada.
Bantam Books, 1540 Broadway, New York, New York 10036.

PRINTED IN THE UNITED STATES OF AMERICA

OPM   10 9 8 7 6 5 4 3 2 1

To Gary, you rogue.
Thanks for the adventure.

ONE

Captain Diego Swift held fast to the massive wooden wheel of his ship, wrestling to steady her bow against the howling force of the hurricane. It was dead certain that she was sinking, the *Mystress* that had served him so well, but Diego refused to let her slip beneath the storm-swept sea until the last of his crew were safely in their lifeboats.

A ship of scoundrels, some would say, who deserved to end up as supper for the sharks. But *Diablo* Swift, the biggest scoundrel of them all, would rather die than leave his loyal men to drown. A decent captain did not abandon the deck of his schooner, no matter how desperate the situation. Of course, in the eyes of polite, nineteenth-century society, Diego the Swashbuckler was far from decent. But even a pirate captain had the right to exit this earth with some shred of honor.

Diego swore viciously as a fifteen-foot wave

dashed over the *Mystress*'s prow, swamping him with a mammoth, foaming wall of warm salt water, leaving him gasping for air. The backwash swirled around his legs, soaking his black leather boots. He kicked them off with an effort, knowing they would work like anchors at his ankles if the next surge succeeded in knocking him overboard.

So much for dying with his boots on. Some damn fools might prefer to meet their end in full dress uniform and sink heroically to the bottom in beautifully garbed glory, but Diego would rather battle it out barefoot to the last. In fact, the idea of dying, no matter how magnificently, didn't much appeal to him at all.

Considering the blackguard's life he'd led up to now, his prospects for a pleasant eternity looked pretty poor. The only way the soul of *Diablo* Swift would enter the pearly gates was if he pried them open himself. Of course, he could always bring Scurvy with him. His first mate had always been good at picking locks . . .

"Bail out, Captain!" a voice shouted behind him. "She's ready to heave. I'll not see you go with her!"

Speak of the devil. Diego turned to see Scurvy clinging to the mainmast like a wharf rat on a dock post, his white hair flying wildly in the wind, a look of fierce determination gleaming dangerously from his sixty-year-old eyes.

"Abandon ship, Scurvy!" Diego commanded, as another wave pounded ruthlessly across the rolling, waterlogged deck. "*Now.*"

"Of course, Cap'n," the first mate called back obediently. "Right after you."

"Bloody *hell*!" Diego cursed at the top of his lungs. "This is no time to argue! Do you think I'd let *you* die on me, old man? Now, be off before it's too late."

The grizzled sailor shook his head obstinately. "Sorry, Your High and Mightiness. I'll lash me brittle bones to the boards if I have to, but I ain't about to leave afore me friend."

"Dammit, mister!" Diego roared into the maelstrom. "This is mutiny. I'll run you through for it!"

"Aye," Scurvy yelled back in agreement, "and so you might. If either of us lives long enough."

Diego felt the *Mystress* plunge heavily to starboard, then bob back up in the roiling whitecaps like a helpless bit of driftwood instead of the sleek and stealthy craft he knew her to be. He had slipped in and out of a hundred ports at her fleet, steady helm and never encountered a storm like this one. The sky had taken on a sickly purple hue, sprouting devil winds, mountainous waves, and stirring up such a sudden, hellish vortex, they were surely in the midst of no ordinary hurricane.

One glance at the horizon and the tall, dark cloud, now twisting toward them, told Diego that the waters ahead would soon grow even deadlier. The tempest had borne a beastly offspring, a black spinning sea-spout which was heading straight for his ship. The funnel-shaped cyclone was approaching so fast, not even the *Mystress* would be able to outrun it.

"Scurvy," Diego urged, his voice hoarse with sudden gravity, "begone with you. The last lifeboat's about to leave."

"So she is," Scurvy noted, "and not enough room on it for the both of us. Take your seat on her, Captain, and let me hold the wheel 'til she's away."

"Never," Diego ground out, ready to haul his old friend over his shoulder and fling him bodily into the lifeboat if necessary.

But he never got the chance. The long tail of the sea twister was already upon them, snapping the mainmast in two, hurling it high in the air, taking the first mate along with it.

"Captain! . . ."

Diego watched in horror as Scurvy was sucked into the whirling airstream a hundred feet above sea level, then dropped again, straight down to the ocean.

"*Scurvy!*" Diego thundered, and dove in after him.

He surfaced to a sky of thick, unforgiving gray with deep blue swells all around him, high and forbidding as fortress walls. The voluminous folds of his fine linen shirt floated upward in the warm, briny water, obscuring his view. Diego tore the garment from his chest, desperately scanning the horizon.

Scurvy was nowhere to be seen.

The lifeboat, too, had disappeared, carried away by the quick-moving currents. Only he and the *Mystress* remained, but the ominous sound of rushing water signaled that she was about to leave him as well.

The buxom wooden maiden carved across her bow was the last thing Diego caught sight of. Her over-size breasts bobbed momentarily against the white peak of a wave, then receded with a final seductive sway beneath the storm-ravaged sea.

Diego threw his head back and cursed the cold, swirling sky. He'd lost his ship, his crew, and his closet friend, all in a matter of seconds.

He was as good as dead himself.

Almost. He tried to get his bearings, but without a single visible star or a straight wind to guide him, he could only guess at the distance and direction of the shore. St. Augustine, his home port, was where he'd been headed when the hurricane hit. To the big beachfront house he'd built there a few years before, the one place on earth he could honestly call his own.

That house was all he had left, now, and Diego promised himself grimly that he *would* set eyes on it again. Peeling his pants off, he tied them into a makeshift sack and began to fill the insides with air, an old sailor's trick that would at least give him something to float on. But he'd only been swimming for a few minutes when the second cyclone hit.

This time Diego felt himself being sucked inside the whirling windstorm. The sound of it was deafening, with the force and fury of a thousand-cannon barrage, every weapon firing at once. He was no more than a speck of gunpowder in the midst of the blast, shooting violently against the funnel walls one second, exploding suddenly outside the next.

Then, as abruptly as it had started, the storm was over.

Diego blinked in astonishment. Where the sea had been churning, it was now as calm as a piece of polished glass. Instead of the night's darkness, there was daybreak. He was no longer many miles out to sea, but merely a few hundred yards from shore. He swam toward it for all he was worth, stumbling onto the beach an hour later, bleary-eyed, half delirious with exhaustion.

In the dim light of dawn, he could just make out the faint, gray outline of his house. Hell, but the hurricane had hit her hard. Broken boards, sagging shutters, peeling paint, all testified to the destructive power of the strange, unnatural turbulence that must have passed through with the storm.

He struggled across the sand toward the house, grateful that it was standing at all. Reaching the front entrance, he soon discovered that although everything else was falling apart, the lock on the door still worked fine. Too bad Scurvy wasn't around to unlatch it for him.

Diego felt the pain of his loss shoot through him, swift and keen as a newly sharpened saber blade. It was *his* fault the loyal old man wasn't here to jimmy the lock open.

But *he* had survived, heaven help him, a half-dead, wet-haired, buck-naked dog of a buccaneer who couldn't even break into his own house. To *hell* with the lock, Diego decided, and kicked the door in with a single wood-splintering blow. Swaggering slowly into the front hall with a smile of bitter satisfaction on his face, he promptly passed out on the floor.

Catalina Steadwell sat bolt upright in bed the minute she heard the sound of the breaking door. With her heart hammering wildly in her throat, she reached for the Saturday night special stowed carefully beneath her pillow. Someone was breaking into her house!

She'd only purchased the old beachfront building three weeks ago, after falling in love with it on sight. The historic St. Augustine neighborhood had seemed safe enough, but she'd bought the gun before moving in, just to make herself feel better. A woman living alone could never be too careful.

Now it seemed that she hadn't been careful enough.

After spending most of her life in small, secure apartments or dorm rooms, she'd acted in haste, buying the ramshackle house on an uncharacteristic impulse. She didn't even have the time to repent her brash venture at leisure. She had to go investigate the sound she'd heard.

Clutching the gun tightly, she made her way out of her bedroom toward the top of the stairs. Maybe it wasn't a break-in or burglary after all. Maybe she just wasn't used to the creaks and clanks and squeaks that a two-hundred-year-old building made. Especially one that was so run-down and in need of restoration.

But as soon as she reached the edge of the landing, she knew her imagination had not been playing tricks on her. Looking down into the front foyer, she instantly ascertained the source of the noise. The door was still ajar. It had definitely been kicked open. Apparently by the man who was lying, motionless, facedown on her floor.

The *naked* man.

Catalina let out a quick gasp at the bare sight of him. What in the world was he doing there? Nothing at the moment, thank goodness. He appeared to be unconscious. Maybe even dead.

But after studying him for another shocked second or two, she was certain she could detect a steady rise and fall motion in the massive breadth of his back. He was breathing. Catalina wasn't sure whether to be relieved by the discovery, or frightened. Alive or not, the stranger had no business being there. Certainly not at five in the morning, wearing nothing but his birthday suit.

It was unsettling enough to have a man break into your house, but a man with no clothes? The sight of it simply defied any calm, rational interpretation Cat could come up with. Worse, there was something about the stranger's sheer, uncensored masculinity that was terrifying and oddly riveting at the same time.

From what she could see of his swarthy, suntanned face and hard-edged features, he was far too rough looking to be attractive. But it wasn't his face she found herself staring at. It was the rest of him.

The windblown mane of blue-black hair that swept down past his jaw, slashing across his shoulders in a dark wave. The endless stretch of muscles. The burnt sienna skin, smattered with sand and sea salt, shaded with the furred, dusky strokes of male body hair. The bold outline of a tattoo etched shamelessly across his backside.

Cat drew in another sharp breath, staring at the inky artwork in involuntary fascination. She couldn't quite make the image out from the safety of her vantage point, but the sight of it still made her wonder. What kind of man would brazenly sport an indelible decoration in such a spot as that? What kind of man would stroll up to her house completely naked, and proceed to bash her door in for no apparent reason?

A dangerous man, Cat decided. Or at the very least, some sicko, exhibitionist pervert who took pleasure in showing himself to defenseless, unwilling women. The kind of lowlife degenerate the world needed far less of.

Carefully cocking the trigger of her gun, Cat crept down the staircase toward him. Luckily, *she* was not defenseless. She would have to call the cops to come and get him, but in the meantime, if there was any saving to be done, Cat knew she'd have to do it herself.

Keeping the barrel of the gun pointed defensively at the man's motionless body, she tiptoed toward him.

"Wake up," she suggested firmly, only half-hoping that he would. An unconscious creep would be much simpler to deal with than one who was fully awake. With any luck, she could just roll his sleeping body right back out the door.

Only, Cat wasn't sure she could budge him by herself. The man looked just too big for her to try to maneuver alone.

"Wake *up*," she insisted again.

The man still didn't move.

Cat leaned a little closer. His broad back was still moving steadily up and down in a slow, rhythmic motion. His breathing was just fine, thank you. It was his hearing that needed help.

Cat turned her gun toward the ceiling. What difference would a little bullet hole make up there, anyway? The plaster was already crumbling away in great, gaping clumps. No one would even notice the mark, but with any luck, the stranger would certainly notice the noise. Being careful to aim clear of the chandelier, she pointed at a stray spot of paint and fired.

The stranger groaned. His eyes flashed open, turning toward Catalina in vague comprehension. "What the devil? . . ."

"My question exactly," Cat finished for him, leveling the gun again squarely at his head. "What the hell are you doing in my house, mister?"

Diego shut his eyes, but the vision of auburn hair and cream-colored lace still floated before him. He opened them again to find an angry vixen who looked ready to kill him with the odd-looking pistol she held in her hand. What had he done to deserve her wrath?

From the fired-up expression on her fair face, it must've been a sin rather awful. Had he bedded her last night and somehow overstayed his welcome? Not likely.

In his experience, women only complained when it was time for him to leave. Complained, coaxed, cajoled, or wept dry tears so that he would stay awhile longer, tossing more of his golden doubloons so generously their way. But not this lovely pistol-toting lass. She clearly wanted him to be gone. He must've done something to set her temper flaring, but he couldn't, for the life of him, remember exactly what.

The only thing he could remember at the moment was the hurricane. The *Mystress* sinking before his eyes. The loss of Scurvy to the sea. Diego groaned again, swearing against the evil forces of fate.

The ornery vixen knelt beside him in her bare feet and pressed the cold metal of her pistol to his forehead. "One more word like that out of your mouth, mister, and you won't be around to regret it. I hear enough rough talk on the streets these days without having to listen to it under my own roof."

Under *her* roof? As Diego's brain began clearing slowly, it occurred to him that Miss Bold-as-Brass was mistaken. This was *his* roof. His house. He could swear up a storm if he wanted to. Of course, it might not be worth having his brains blown out, but didn't a man have a right to speak freely on his own property?

"Have a care there, sweet," he cautioned her. "Why not talk first, postpone your shooting until later?"

"Smooth talk won't help you any more than swearing," she promised him. "And I am not your *sweet*, sicko. Try Catalina Steadwell, instead. That's Cat to my friends, Ms. Steadwell to you."

"Sicko?" Diego repeated, puzzled. "Aye, Miss Catalina, I *am* feeling poorly. My head is swimming, my throat dry. Would you mind, lass, if I sit up for a moment?"

"As a matter of fact," she informed him, "I mind very much. Haven't you had enough cheap thrills for one morning without subjecting me to the full show?"

Diego's head was way past swimming by now and well on its way to aching sorely. Surely the woman beside him was no vixen, but hell's gatekeeper sent to torture him for the wayward, roguish life he'd led. The flashes of red flame in her auburn hair should've warned him from the start. But the cool, melodic voice had lured him in, compelling as a siren's song.

What thrills was she speaking of anyway? Unfortunately, he hadn't had any of those for nearly a month now. Show? What show? Did she have to talk to him in riddles? He was too bloody tired to play the lady's game, too bloody thirsty and cold.

Cold? Hell, he was shaking all the way to his bones in the sea-damp air of the summer morning.

Glancing down, Diego suddenly realized what might have Miss Catalina Steadwell so fired up and flustered.

He hadn't any clothes on. He'd washed ashore this way, wet and naked as a sunburnt ship rat. He hadn't made it to bed with Miss Steadwell, or anyone else for that matter. Aye, and a crying shame it was, for she looked like just the type of woman that a man might find comfort in when he needed it most.

She was sleekly built, with skin the color of sunwashed seashells and wide copper eyes, deep enough to fathom his soul. And a body sensual enough to make a man forget. Judging by the short, provocative chemise she wore, that was exactly what she might've done for him. Right before he'd keeled over, which would explain his sudden memory loss. Diego was heartily sorry he'd missed the moment. Was there no end to the misery fate had wrought for him?

"You're shaking," she said, her voice softer.

"Aye," Diego responded, "like a leaf."

"More like the whole tree," she observed dryly. "Are you really ill?"

"Sick with fear," he said, and flashed her an easy grin. "I'm rather partial to my forehead, sweet, and would as soon not lose it. It's one of my better parts."

Catalina couldn't stop herself from responding to the stranger's unexpected sense of humor. The man had guts, she had to give him that. He was prone and vulnerable, and he still had the nerve to be cocky.

And how many sickos came with a smile that could steal your breath away? So maybe he wasn't *all* bad.

She backed off a few feet and loosened her grip on the gun. "Believe me, bub, it's the only part I want to see right now. If I get a blanket, will you promise to cover everything else up with it?"

He nodded. "Of course, Catalina, until you ask otherwise. But I am not bub."

Unwilling to turn her back on him, Cat lifted a patchwork quilt from its spot on the couch and gingerly tossed it his way. "Not—well, no, I didn't imagine that was your real name."

"I am Diego Swift," he told her, standing up slowly as he covered himself with the quilt, tying the ends at his waist in a neat, intricate knot.

"Oh?" Catalina's eyebrows went up, and she nodded politely, but her mouth had gone suddenly dry. Not at the name he had spoken so proudly, but at the sight of him towering over her. A prone, helpless pervert was one thing, but upright, Diego Swift appeared to be neither. Rather, he exuded male prowess and cool self-assurance along every streamlined inch of him. The sharp, confident curve of his shoulders, the commanding set of his jaw, the clear look of interest in his bold blue eyes that was beginning to border on insolence . . .

Cat watched him cross to her couch and lean against it expectantly. She could swear there was a hint of a swagger in his walk. Any man who could move that way while wearing a wedding-ring pattern of floral cotton calico was clearly a character to be reckoned with. But Cat had no desire to reckon with Mr. Diego Swift.

She swallowed hard, more grateful than ever that she hadn't seen him *completely* naked. And what was that shiny thing in his right ear? A golden hoop? An *earring*? No, she'd definitely seen *enough*.

"Well then, Mr. Swift—"

"Captain," he corrected her.

"I beg your pardon?"

"It's Captain Swift," he stated emphatically.

"Oh . . . Captain? Of what?" she joked. "A federation starship? Did you graduate first in your class at Starfleet Academy?"

A puzzled frown came over his stubble-rough face. "I do not know this Starfleet. I am—was—captain of the *Mystress*—a fine ship which sank last night in the hurricane. My crew has disappeared—I don't know where. My first mate drowned . . . I alone made it to shore alive. To this house. *My* house, which, miraculously has weathered the worst storm of this century."

Catalina was shocked into silence. It was no use demanding a sane explanation for what he was really doing there because the poor man was undoubtedly crackers. He obviously believed the things he was saying, things that Cat knew couldn't possibly be true. For starters, last night was one of the balmiest they'd had the entire month of August. There had been no hurricane. No storm of the century.

And the only thing this house had weathered for the last thirty years or so was vandalism and sheer neglect. She was also completely positive about just *who* it belonged to. Every rotting, sagging, leaking, squeaking square foot of it.

She still wasn't entirely sure why she'd been so drawn to the place. The building had been run-down, abandoned, and battered by time, but there was a hauntingly beautiful quality about it, even in its current state, that had struck a vulnerable chord in Cat's heart. A chord that went even deeper than her fascination for days gone by which had led to her career as a local historian.

It was the stability of the structure that had appealed to her even more than the neglected beauty of the house. The simple, comforting idea of a home that had lasted, enduring in spite of the ravages the years had wrought. To Cat, who had never had a real home, never known the security of a loving family, the permanence of the place was its most wonderful quality. A place she could finally call her own.

The old house had roots that went deep, like a withered rosebush sagging under the weight of a winter snow. A rosebush with the potential to bloom again given the right kind of care.

Cat had vowed to give it that care, to do her best to restore it to its former glory, but so far her best hadn't been good enough. In spite of the preservation plan she'd put together to get the house listed in the National Register of Historic Places, her proposal and request for grant monies had been denied. The structure had undergone too many architectural additions and changes over the years to meet the strict guidelines required for federal or state approval.

Unfortunately, she'd already sunk nearly every penny of her life savings into the house just to keep it standing. The basic structural repairs alone had far exceeded the engineer's early estimates. And she still needed outside funding to complete the project.

But her renovation problems seemed small at the moment compared to those of the man in front of her. How was she going to bring him back to reality? Was it better to humor his delusions, or confront them head-on?

"Captain," she began cautiously, "the weather was lovely last night."

"Lovely?" he repeated, incredulous. "Lovely if you like dervishes and disasters, lass. Just look around you at the condition my house is in. Nay, she didn't get this way from a balmy breeze blowing in from the south. She looks as though she's had the guts ripped right out of her!"

"Well, yes," Cat agreed. "But what do you expect from a building that's nearly two hundred years old?"

Diego stared at her. Blue eyes, Cat noticed. As deep and aquamarine as the depths of a sunlit ocean.

"Two hundred years?" he demanded. "Catalina, my lady, I'm afraid you're one sail short of a full set. I had this house built only three years ago."

Cat resisted the urge to press her hand against Diego Swift's sun-touched forehead and check for signs of a fever. "What year would that be, exactly?"

she asked him, hoping simple logic would be suffi-
cient to get her point across. The building clearly
dated from the time of St. Augustine's second Spanish regime, not from the late twentieth century.
Surely, any lunatic could see that. But then, "Captain" Swift was not just any lunatic.

"Why, 1807, of course" was his unexpected answer.

Cat felt an uneasy tickle move slowly down her
spine. How had he pinpointed the time so precisely?
No one would be likely to know such an obscure
detail about her house unless they had done some
research—and Diego didn't look like the type of guy
who'd spent a lot of time in libraries. Something very
weird was going on.

"So this year," she prompted, "the date would
be—1810?"

"Aye, lass, last time I looked."

Cat's fears were confirmed. He actually believed
he was living in the early nineteenth century! Of
course, he was crazy. Way off the deep end. But the
realization brought more than mere pity for the man.
It was disconcerting to Cat as well.

She would have to ask him to leave. At least, she
should, especially since she *knew* what a mental mess
the "Captain" really was. Still, she'd always been a
sucker for hard-luck cases, and this mixed-up, homeless man was obviously that.

Only, he didn't exactly strike her as the kind of
man who'd completely lost his own self-identity and
ego. He seemed to have plenty of the latter, in fact,

which only made the tragedy of his situation that much more poignant.

"Eighteen-ten," Cat repeated, keeping the level of her voice low and calm for his sake. She hated to be the one to have to set him straight, but surely someone should. Maybe hearing the truth would help snap him out of it.

"Captain," she continued, trying to be kind, yet firm, "I'm afraid your dates are a little off. Nearly two centuries off, in fact. The current year is 1998."

His dark blue eyes scanned her with slow intensity, as though *she* was the one who'd really lost her mind. Clearly, he didn't believe her.

"Never mind," she said, trying to soothe him. "You're obviously in denial."

"Denial!" he thundered. "Of course I deny it, lass. Do you not believe I know what year it is?"

Catalina waved the gun again in warning. "Don't step over the edge on me here, Captain. I'm only trying to help, but if you get out of line again, I'll have to ask you to leave."

"Leave my own house? Woman, it's you who's gone mad. I don't take orders from anyone!" He turned his back on her as soon as he'd spoken, folding his arms across his chest, effectively dismissing her.

"Wanna bet?" she asked, taking strategic aim at the Captain's quilt-covered backside. "I'm a pretty fair shot with this thing. I can probably hit that tattoo of yours with my eyes closed."

Diego whipped back around, staring in fascination at the weapon she held in her hand. "What is the name of that pistol you are holding, Catalina?"

"This thing?" she asked him. "Oh, of course, being from the nineteenth century, you've obviously never seen one before. It's euphemistically referred to as a 'Saturday night special.' Unfortunately, there's nothing special about it. It's just a common handgun."

The color was starting to drain from the captain's face, turning the burnished metal skin from sun-drenched copper to a cool, ashen gray. "A hand . . . gun?"

Feeling responsible for the sudden change in Swift's complexion, Catalina felt instantly guilty. She hadn't meant to terrorize the unfortunate man, but she did have a perfect right to protect herself.

"Right," she answered gently. "The weapon of choice for a modern woman like me."

But if Swift had been startled by her gun, he lost interest in it just as quickly. His attention shifted entirely to her, and the skimpy summer nightie Cat was wearing.

"Modern?" he asked, checking her and the lace outfit over with a thoroughness that could only be described as audacious. He reached out without warning, boldly taking the hem of her skirt and proceeding to test the material with a sharp tug. "Is this something modern women wear, Catalina? Nay, you had me confounded for a minute there with the oddness of your pistol, but nothing about your garment would give a man cause to worry or complain."

Catalina's jaw dropped, and her face flushed hot with indignation. She might've admired his nerve if she hadn't been so taken aback by it. Regardless, Cat took the cocky gesture as her cue to call it quits with the captain. Being nice to some lost, stranded soul was one thing, putting up with his outrageous, provocative behavior another. She wanted him *out, now!*

Slapping his hand away, she poked the barrel of her gun straight into his rock-hard abdomen and backed him slowly toward the door. "That's it, bub," she assured him. "No more Ms. Nice Gal. It's time for you to take a hike."

"A hike?" he asked, apparently confused.

But Cat wasn't feeling too sympathetic to his disorientation any longer. "Leave," she amended. "It's simple, Swift. All you have to do is turn around and walk out the door."

"But, Catalina—"

"Now," she insisted.

Reluctantly, he turned to face the front doorway, which was still thrown open to the street beyond. A busy street by now. Cars were beginning to whiz past on their way to work. A jogger dashed by in neon yellow sweats as a jet rumbled noisily overhead. The paperboy rode toward them and hurled the plastic-wrapped morning news onto Cat's front porch.

Diego Swift stopped dead in his tracks. He glanced around slowly at the traffic-filled street, the roaring, smoking sky, the paper at his feet with the date printed clearly in the upper-right-hand corner. He didn't bother to read it. He didn't have to.

The words were growing too damn blurry to make out anyway, along with everything else around him. The floor itself seemed to be spinning before his eyes, moving toward his face as the ground rushed up to meet him.

TWO

"Dehydration," Cat's plumber pronounced after checking out Diego's vital signs with an experienced eye. "What this boy needs is water."

"Are you sure?" Cat asked, staring down at the captain's unconscious body as a wave of guilt washed over her. It was her fault he'd fainted.

He *had* said something about being thirsty, but she'd completely ignored it, not even offering him what she would've gone out of her way to give a stray dog. The Sisters of Mercy would've shaken their fingers at her for such shameful conduct, and for once, Cat wouldn't blame them. The nuns at the convent boarding school had spent years enumerating her seemingly endless faults, but it had taken less than an hour with this stranger to make her feel ashamed of herself.

So much for the grandiose plans she'd once made for saving the world. She couldn't even save one weak, tired, most likely homeless man from passing out right in front of her.

Luckily, O'Massey had shown up on her doorstep only minutes after Diego's fall, and instantly assessed the situation.

"Boyfriend been out drinkin' on you? Poor sucker looks to be in pretty bad shape."

Cat turned red to the roots of her hair. She'd been too busy worrying about the captain's appearance in her house to predict the shape he was really in.

"I don't know *what's* wrong with him," she confessed, reluctant to admit just how unfamiliar she was with the half-naked man on her floor. She was still wearing her nightie, for heaven's sake. She knew how it must look. But it seemed foolish to waste time explaining.

Thank goodness O'Massey was quicker to come up with a prognosis than he normally was while tinkering over her rusty pipes.

"Been in that sort of shape myself a few times, and there's only one cure. Liquids, and lots of 'em. Bring me a pitcher of water and we'll see if we can pour some down his throat."

Being careful to hide the gun from O'Massey's sight, Cat headed for the kitchen, wondering if it wouldn't be wiser to call in some qualified medical help. But it might well take forever just to get anyone to show up, and when they finally did arrive, it was easy to guess where the captain would be sailing off to. Straitjacket city.

One earful of that story he'd concocted and the asylum authorities would lock him up and throw away the key. He'd be at the mercy of the state, the mercy of strangers, an intolerable situation as far as Cat was concerned. Orphaned at six, she knew what it was like to be totally alone, with no immediate family to depend on.

Terrifying. Traumatic.

The illegitimate child of two free-thinking hippies, she'd been more or less on her own from the day her idealistic parents had died in a car accident. Unfortunately, Rainbow-Painter and Mountain Woman had never imagined they would both lose their lives so suddenly, or that their only daughter would end up a ward of the state. Loved by no one.

But that's the way it had been for Cat. Her unmarried parents hadn't believed they needed a piece of paper to prove their love, nor had they left any legal documents that would provide for her.

The Sisters of Mercy at the convent had been good enough to take her into their boarding school for girls. They just hadn't had room enough to take her into their hearts.

That kind of fate was something she wouldn't wish on anyone, not even a half-crazed stranger like Captain Swift. No, especially not someone like him. The man had enough machismo in his little finger to crush rocks. If a guy with that much brawn and brute strength was forced to relinquish control of his life—well, it wouldn't be a pretty sight. If there was any way to prevent it, Cat promised herself she would.

"I hope you know what you're doing," she warned O'Massey, handing him a full pitcher of water on her way back into the foyer. "We definitely don't want to make him any worse."

"Don't worry about it, lady," he reassured her. "I'm a master plumber, aren't I? Now you hold his head while I pour."

Reluctantly, Cat crouched down beside the captain and cautiously put her hand to his face. The angle of his jaw was blunt and hard beneath her fingers, the burnished skin rough with stubble but surprisingly warm. Male body heat. Diego Swift gave off enough of it to melt steel. A good sign, Cat decided, carefully tipping his chin back. At least he wasn't in shock.

Unfortunately, she couldn't say the same thing. The flesh across her fingertips was beginning to burn—not with heat, but with an erotic awareness of the man beneath. Sensual awareness of a man she had no business feeling attracted to. A perfect stranger.

Appalled, Cat snatched her hand away. She could only imagine what the nuns would have to say about her now. Being branded from the start as a child of "free love," she'd never had the chance to meet with the strict sisters' approval. She'd tried to live up to their lofty standards, but after spending the first six years of her life in a setting with few restrictions, it was nearly impossible to remember all of the stringent new rules at once. She'd been punished so many times that first year at school, her knuckles had grown callused from the repeated raps of the teachers' rulers.

But Cat had learned her lesson well. She'd learned to hide her impulsive side, carefully disciplining herself to fight against any forbidden feelings that could get her into further trouble.

The nuns, unfortunately, had believed the change they saw in her was too little, too late. Her current behavior would only confirm that Catalina Steadwell had a streak of sinful curiosity a mile wide. A wild, willful streak that refused to be rubbed out no matter how hard they tried.

Cat couldn't bring herself to acknowledge the possibility that they might've been right. Was it so wicked of her to respond instinctively to a man she'd only met this morning, to wonder what it would be like to . . . ? Okay, so maybe she'd strayed toward the sinful side for a moment. But having certain thoughts and acting on them were two entirely different things. It would be easier to keep her mind on track if she kept her hands off Swift.

Easier said than done.

"A little farther back," O'Massey suggested, positioning the spout of the pitcher just a few inches high of the captain's parted lips. "Look, lady, are you going to help me out here, or not?"

"Sorry," Cat murmured, steadying Swift's head again.

Diego's reaction to the liquid pouring down his throat was immediate. He came to, coughing violently, with lethal speed. Before Cat realized what was happening, he was lunging for O'Massey, and knocking the surprised plumber to the floor.

"Stop!" Cat cried. "You'll kill him."

"Aye," Diego agreed, "and why shouldn't I? The scoundrel tried to choke me. What are you after, bilge-breath?" he demanded, wrapping his massive hands around O'Massey's thick neck and starting to squeeze.

The plumber spluttered weakly as his face turned red.

"*Stop it*," Cat repeated firmly, really starting to fear for O'Massey's life. The man's eyes were fairly popping out of his head by now, while Diego's enormous biceps were barely bulging from the effort. "You don't understand. He was only trying to help."

Diego's rock-hard hold on the plumber began to relax. "Help what, Catalina? Help you drown me?"

"Of course not," she responded softly. "You were out cold, remember? We were hoping the water would revive you."

He glanced briefly down at the blue-faced O'Massey. "Is that so, mate?"

His victim nodded vigorously.

Diego relinquished him with a hearty slap on the shoulder. "Sorry, friend," he said, standing.

The plumber rolled onto his back, gasping for air. "Sure—thing," he managed, holding his hands to his throat as if to make sure it was still there.

"You okay?" Cat asked him.

"Fine, lady," the plumber coughed, struggling to

his feet. "Just fine. But I've suddenly remembered an appointment on the other side of town. See ya."

Seconds later, he was out the door.

Cat spun around, glaring at Diego. "He's never coming back, you know. A month on his waiting list, no working bathtub in the whole house, and the odds of ever seeing him again are slim to none."

Diego shrugged, the look on his face not the least bit apologetic. "Want me to fetch him back for you, Catalina?"

"No, thanks!" she responded quickly, knowing he could easily accomplish the task if he tried. "You've done enough already. And I'd just as soon not have to bail you out of jail for assault and battery."

Reaching for the pitcher of water that, miraculously, had landed upright on the floor, Diego downed the contents in one long, satisfying swig. "Better than rum," he told her, wiping the moisture from his mouth with a careless swipe against one well-muscled shoulder.

"Rum?" she asked suspiciously, wondering if O'Massey had been right about the captain's condition after all. "Is that why you passed out? Were you drunk?"

He tossed the empty pitcher onto a drop-cloth-covered table and flashed her a wicked smile. "Nay, lass, and more's the pity. Had I been drunk," he confided, "I would never have taken a tumble. No, Catalina, it's this century of yours that has me seeing stars. Stars and speeding carriages and a jolting, jarring jumble of chaos and confusion." The blue eyes locked boldly with hers. "And visions I could never have imagined in my sweetest midnight dreams."

Catalina's breath caught. Lord help her, but for a serious psychiatric candidate, the man certainly was smooth. As a bandit. One look into those cool, Caribbean-blue eyes and he could easily steal a woman's heart away. Any woman's, Cat amended, except hers. Still, there wasn't much she could do to stop him from *trying* . . .

With a single step of his long legs, he closed the distance between them, crowding her up against the back of the couch as he took her small chin in his hand and tilted her face toward him. "Tell me, woman," he demanded softly, his voice low and sexy enough to make any good Catholic girl's knees weak. "Am I dreaming?"

With the same courage that had served Cat well in her difficult convent school days, and helped her establish a comfortable career as a historian, she steeled herself to resist this assault on her senses. It wasn't easy with a man whose mere physical presence was enough to make the room temperature rise by ten degrees.

And Cat definitely felt the heat skyrocketing inside her. Her breathing quickened, and her nostrils filled with the scent of him. He smelled of the ocean, of briny salt spray and sun-warmed skin and the adventurous essence of male. He smelled *sexy*, for heaven's sake.

"Dreaming?" Cat repeated lightly, ducking nimbly away from Diego's unnerving reach and folding her arms in front of her. "I'm afraid the accurate term for it is hallucinating."

Diego grinned back in undisguised approval. She was a tough little thing, he had to give her that. The kind of woman who could lead him on a merry chase to bed and back again, as long as he cared to follow. That was one thing, at least, the centuries hadn't changed. He did still care to follow. But Catalina Steadwell was only one piece of the puzzle that fate had put before him. A complex knot that even an experienced captain like himself would have a hard time unraveling.

Ocean squalls, enemy ships, sharks, black island magic, they were nothing compared to the unlucky hand last night's hurricane had dealt him. He was at a loss to explain it, but somehow that storm had tossed him forward in time.

Worse, Miss Steadwell did not believe him. Not that he could blame her entirely. It was a tall tale that stretched the bounds of credibility to the breaking point. But he was a man used to being taken at his word. Very few men, in fact, had ever questioned his authority up till now. At least none that had lived to repeat themselves.

But in the course of the last two hundred years or so, his house had somehow fallen into the hands of Catalina Steadwell, leaving his current fate there as well. And for the first time in his life, Captain Diego Swift, undisputed head plunderer of the high seas, commander of more than a hundred fierce-hearted, freebooting buccaneers, the most feared, cheered, and revered rogue of his day, was expected to explain himself to a wench.

It was an idea that, like this strange new century he found himself in, would take some getting used to.

"A lunatic, am I?" he asked her.

"More like a *dangerous* lunatic," she amended.

"Could be," he admitted. "I've been called worse. But you have nothing to fear from me, Catalina. I've never hurt a woman in my life."

"In that case," she responded dryly, "feel free to make yourself at home."

Taking her at her word, Diego sank back against the worn couch cushions and proceeded to stretch out. He was sore and tired from all that swimming. A few hours' rest was what he needed to put the wind back into his sails. With any luck, he would wake up on board the *Mystress* again and discover that the year 1998 was no more than a distant nightmare . . .

His eyes hadn't been closed for more than a second or two when her voice sounded behind him.

"What do you think you're doing?"

Diego didn't bother to crack an eyelid.

"I'm *sleeping*, Catalina," he responded sternly. "At least I would be if you saw fit to lower your voice to the decibel of distant cannon fire."

"I beg your pardon?" she breathed.

"My pardon is granted," Diego told her magnanimously. "Just see that it doesn't happen again."

"Oh, it *won't*," Cat assured him. "I can promise you that. Because you were just about to be leaving."

Diego opened one eye, surprised at the anger in her voice. Aye, she was furious all right. Her copper eyes were flashing fiercely down at him from above, the expression on her face so enraged, she was close to spitting fire. He wasn't sure what he'd done to provoke her, but that didn't stop him from taking in the sights.

The woman was more than a puzzle to him. With her nostrils flaring and her auburn hair flaming against the creamy, lace-covered shoulders, she was a tempting whirlwind of pent-up passion. The idea of sleeping was swept suddenly to the back of Diego's mind, only to be replaced by a stronger, more pressing desire. Very pressing, considering the recent month he'd spent at sea without a single stop in port. No, leaving was the last thing Diego wanted to do at the moment, no matter how fond Miss Steadwell might be of the idea.

"And just where would you expect me to go, lass?" he demanded. "I've nothing to my name at the moment. No currency or coin, no acquaintances, no clothes. Would you be cold enough to throw a man out onto the street in such circumstances?"

Catalina hesitated. Would she? Damn the infernal man for confusing the issue, anyway. What was she supposed to do? Let him hang around wearing nothing but a quilt, making himself comfortable on her furniture while he ordered her about? No thank you. He was simply asking too much.

"Sorry, Captain," she told him, "but I'm not running a boardinghouse here. If it's cash and clothes you're looking for, I can spare twenty bucks and a pair of overalls the painter left in the attic. Take it or leave it."

The puzzled frown returned to his face. "Bucks and overalls, Catalina? Are you making me a generous offer?"

"Let's just say it's my *only* offer," Cat quipped, crooking her finger at him. "Come on. I'll show you."

The stairs were blessedly silent as Cat wound her way up to the third-story attic, but the way the floorboards squeaked and groaned from Diego's passage reminded Cat of a book she'd once read about spirit-haunted houses and the noisy, havoc-wreaking ghosts that stirred inside them, refusing to leave. *He* reminded her of one of those ghosts.

Only, Swift was very much alive. Cat couldn't forget that for a minute, no matter how much she wanted to. He wouldn't let her.

"Why are we stopping here, Catalina?" he called behind her as their progress came to a halt on the second-story landing. "I thought you were taking me to the attic. This is the bedroom."

Cat spun around to face him. Exactly how had he known that? Her bedroom door was partway open, but no furnishings could be seen from where he stood. In fact, the only piece of furniture in the whole room was the marvelous, massive antique bed that had somehow survived with the house. A wrought-iron masterpiece of Spanish design that at the moment was hidden from view.

"Lucky guess," she commented. "Wait here. I just want to grab a robe."

She was back on the landing a moment later, wrapping the oversize terry-cloth garment around her and tying the ends in a secure knot. There. Maybe that's what had been bothering her the whole morning. It was impossible to maintain any kind of authority over an intruder when you were wearing a next-to-nothing summer nightie.

Authority? Who was she kidding? Swift wasn't going to relinquish a teaspoon of that to her. He shook his head slowly, glancing down at her with a look of distinct disappointment in his cool aquamarine eyes. "If this is what women of the day are wearing," he commented, "I am ready to be sent back to my own century."

"Don't tempt me," Catalina said smoothly. "And you're not exactly making a fashion statement yourself in that quilt there, Captain." What did she care what the raffish roughneck thought about her outfit, anyway?

"Since you seem to know your way around the house so well," Cat continued, "you can take the lead up to the attic."

"Of course."

But as soon as he started climbing the stairs again, Cat became aware of her tactical mistake. No, she could see it clearly now. She should never, never have let the captain lead the way. It was the view from behind that really brought it home to her. That swagger in his walk, that cocky, I'm-in-control-here strut that spoke volumes about Swift's current state of mind.

Dammit, but he was enjoying himself.

And he seemed to know exactly where he was going. Not that it took any great powers of deduction to figure out which direction the attic was in, but there was a familiar confidence in the way he took the staircase curves that hinted he'd been there before.

Cat felt the goose bumps beginning to rise along her arm in spite of the heavy robe she was wearing. It wasn't possible that he really had lived in the house at some other time.

Was it?

He disappeared inside the third-story room, smoothly ducking his head to avoid contact with the six-foot doorjamb. Cat followed closely behind.

In spite of its distant location and decrepit condition, this was far and away her favorite part of the house. The space was more than ample, stretching the entire length of the building in one direction, to the edge of the high roof eaves in the other. The floorboards were dark with the dust of two centuries, the corners cluttered with the discards of days gone by, but there was a crumbling beauty about the enormous room that had somehow been enhanced by the haze of time.

Here, it was easy for Cat to escape the noise and chaos of the street below and seek a peaceful, secret sanctuary in the historical ambience she loved so well. Characters from the past came alive for her in this ramshackle room. What fashionably dressed lady had occupied that desk by the large picture window, staring dreamily out over the ocean as she penned exquisite poetry across a gilt-edged page in flowing script? What successful male merchant had stood by that same window, hands clasped impatiently behind him, as he waited for his silk-, spice-, and silver-laden trading ship to come sailing into the harbor?

And now Swift was asking her to believe that *he* had once occupied that same vantage point? Cat couldn't quite get used to the idea. For starters, Diego Swift was a far cry from the elegant, finely clad historical figures she'd dreamed up to fit her beloved setting. With that long sweep of hair flowing out from behind, the island-dark skin set off by the glint of gold at his ear, and the rakish tattoo that still lurked somewhere beneath the makeshift cotton kilt, he fit the part of a smuggler much more closely than that of a somber sea captain.

But just when she was starting to convince herself that a tough, roguish character like Swift clearly didn't belong there, he strolled to the wide casement window, popped the paint-covered latch to the up position with a single, smooth flick of his wrist, and threw the panes open to the fresh air outside.

Cat couldn't believe it. She'd been trying to pry that stubborn latch loose for almost a week, but hadn't managed to budge it more than a millimeter. Even Walt, the part-time painter, had given up on it in frustration after hammering away at the permanently fused metal for nearly an hour. "Stuck fast," he'd told her, and proceeded to work around it.

"I don't know how you managed that," she admitted, "but the fresh air sure feels good. Thanks."

He turned back toward her, raking a shock of streaming black hair from his eyes. The smile on his face was amused, as warm and easy as the afternoon breeze that was beginning to blow in from the ocean. "You're welcome, Catalina. But why don't you have a man around the house to do these simple things for you?"

The sudden question left her struggling for an answer. "I—It's really none of your business, Captain," she shot back defensively.

He cocked a shoulder at her. "If you say so."

"I don't need a man," she added in irritation. "I'm doing just fine on my own."

The all-seeing blue eyes glanced doubtfully around the decaying, dilapidated room. "Are you?" he inquired, with that cut-to-the-chase directness that was nearly impossible to ignore.

"Okay, so I'll admit the house isn't exactly in mint condition. But I'm fixing it up. Gradually. And I can always hire out what I can't handle myself."

If she could only get the funding for it, that is. Since she'd already been turned down at the federal and state levels, a grant from the local preservation league was the only hope she had left. Unfortunately, the St. Augustine Beautification Board was made up entirely of blue-haired blue bloods who seemed more interested in local gossip than local history. Winning over their approval in the upcoming meeting was going to take nothing short of a minor miracle, especially since she had less than a week to get the house in order for their visit. But she would simply have to face that problem when she came to it. Meanwhile, she had the captain to contend with.

She spotted the overalls, still draped across the wooden ladder where the painter had left them. "There," she told Diego, pointing to the sturdy, oversize pants sewn from white cotton canvas. "Walt usually keeps a clean pair around to change into. This must be your lucky day."

"Breeches made of sailcloth?" he asked skeptically.

"Better than a skirt," she reminded him.

"Aye," he agreed shortly, starting to shed the cumbersome confines of the quilt without further argument.

"Wait!" Cat protested, covering her eyes. "Jeez, didn't anyone ever teach you the concept of modesty?"

His laugh was low, rusty, sensual enough to make Cat blink at the sound of it. "Modest?" he asked doubtfully. "No one has ever accused me of being that."

Opening her eyes again, Cat discovered with some relief that he was fully dressed. Well, if not *fully*, at least he had managed to slip those absurdly powerful legs of his into the overalls and cover the rest of himself to the waist. It didn't really matter that the bib was doubled over at the beltline, leaving his chest as exposed as ever. It was the way the material tugged at his muscles that gave her pause, the way the seams stretched and strained against the mountainous, marble-hard thighs that made her marvel.

She had always believed Walt to be a big man. Compared to the captain, he was downright puny.

It really was a shame, she decided, for a body like that to go to waste. Why not, she wondered, give all those marvelous, capable muscles of his a higher purpose in life? Why not put him to work?

"Captain," she said, "are you as good with a hammer and nail as you are with jammed windows?"

"Good enough," he agreed.

"Have you ever held down a steady job?"

"Steady? Nay, Catalina. Never."

"But you are out of work, now?"

"Aye. My livelihood has sunk, you might say."

"Because I was just thinking, how would you like to come to work for me? Odd jobs, fixing up the house, that sort of thing. I can't pay very much, but at least it would give you something."

He ran a hand across the six-o'clock shadow on his chin, considering. "It isn't currency I'm needing. It's room and board."

Cat shook her head slowly. "I'm afraid that's impossible. I can't let you stay here. Besides, there isn't enough room. The guest bedroom isn't even livable yet."

"This space would be fine," he suggested. "For now."

"Oh, I don't think so," Cat told him. "There are other issues involved besides sleeping arrangements. Safety issues—that sort of thing."

"No need to worry about that, Catalina. I can keep you safe—from anything."

"Oh! Actually, what I meant was . . ." Cat didn't have the nerve to tell him that *he* posed the greatest threat to her welfare at the moment.

But, on second thought, having a reckless-looking, earring-clad brigand like him around might have beneficial side effects she hadn't previously considered. Like seriously discouraging anybody else from breaking into her home. With a built-in ruffian like Diego living in the house, she wouldn't be such an easy target. At least having a man hanging around the place would make her feel safer.

They didn't need to know that the captain was probably just some harmless, homeless man with no other place to live. Yes, harmless, she reassured herself. If he'd had any plans to molest her, he would've done his worst by now, wouldn't he?

"Come to think of it," she told him, "maybe we can work something out. On a trial basis."

"So I can stay, then, Catalina? I have your word?"

"You'll have to earn your keep," she warned him.

"I'll do my best."

"No funny business, or you're out on your—tat-too."

"Aye."

"There's a folding cot around here, somewhere. You can sleep on that."

Diego began rummaging for it in a pile of junk in the corner, but only succeeded in producing an old spyglass, tarnished with age, an outdated TV, which he seemed to be fascinated with, and a long metal sword of some kind with a wicked-looking blade.

He ran his finger reverently along the point where the tip had turned a dark reddish-brown.

"Rust," she warned him. "I hope you've had a tetanus shot. The salt air eats everything around here."

He shook his head with a smile. "Nay, Miss Steadwell. That's not rust you're seeing. It's blood."

Cat swallowed hard, staring down at the caked and crusted iron edge where the captain still held it. "Blood?"

"The blood of a greedy, bloated Spaniard who wasn't satisfied with the shipload of gold he had stolen from the Maya. He wanted my ship as well, and my head for a souvenir."

"Your—head?"

"Aye. And a hefty price there was on it at the time. But you'll be noticing I didn't give it to him. I borrowed this bit of blood from him, instead."

"A price on your head?" Cat repeated quietly. "Just what kind of captain do you think you are?"

The sword caught the light as he tested it in the air, slashing the stillness with a single swift stroke of his wrist. Satisfied with the weapon's superior performance, he lowered it with a flourish and turned toward her. His smile was bold, breathtaking. Deadly.

"Why, a pirate captain, of course, my lovely Catalina. Did I fail to mention it?"

THREE

Television, Diego decided, was a marvelous modern invention. With such an amazing device, a man could travel to any number of different places without once having to leave his home port. Nay, it was even better than that. With this sort of miraculous magic at hand, he didn't even have to leave his own bed.

A bloody, infernal invention. Of what use was an adventurer like himself in an age where voyaging itself was undertaken so easily? Surely a contraption of this kind was enough to put a pirate out of work.

Kicking back on his attic cot, he flipped impatiently through the pictures with the aid of the small rectangular instrument Catalina had given him.

Pirate. Now there was a word he hadn't heard mentioned yet on a single television *station*. It didn't even seem to be in use in the English language any longer.

No wonder Catalina hadn't been the least bit impressed by his previous occupation. True, the sight of the blood had sent her swaying for a second there, but she had rallied at an alarmingly rapid rate. Didn't the woman realize what kind of man he was?

In his day, the reputation of *Diablo* Swift had been enough to strike terror in the hearts of men and make women weak at the knees. Just weak enough to tumble willingly into bed with him. This woman, unfortunately, showed no such signs of feminine frailty.

It was a new experience for a man like him to have a member of the fairer sex resist him so thoroughly. Finding himself thrown inexplicably into this new century was challenging enough. But the way Catalina coolly managed to face him without fainting, or worse, without falling headlong into the hay with him, was even more confounding.

The audacious woman still intended to put him to work in his own house. And what choice did he have but to agree to her terms? He needed Miss Steadwell's, correction, *Ms.* Steadwell's help to maneuver the unfamiliar waters he found himself in.

The late twentieth century had surprises in store for him around every corner. The *day off* she'd given him to recuperate from the shipwreck had been enough to show him that. A walk down the street and a few hours spent in front of the television had clued him in.

Indeed, the customs of this century were strange. Disputes were no longer settled by swordplay. The popular custom of lawsuits had taken the place of a meeting at dawn on the field of honor, a cowardly way of settling things to Diego's way of thinking. Small cards of a substance called plastic seemed to be far more valuable than gold. And women had become too damned independent for their own britches.

Especially Cat Steadwell, the spitfire spinster who now held the deed to his house. While he was kicking his heels in the attic, she was sleeping in his bedroom, as peaceful as you please. Without him.

Didn't the maddening minx know what she was missing?

Apparently not. From the saucy, take-charge way she had of ordering him about, she had long since forgotten what women like her were made for.

Pleasure.

Aye, and he would be more than willing to give her plenty of it, if he could only get her to cut him some slack. Unfortunately, the headstrong female had taken it into her mind that odd jobs and domestic duties around the house would somehow do him good. But the only sort of domestic duties that *Diablo* Swift was cut out to perform were those that took place in the bedroom. Somehow, he intended to prove that to the overconfident Catalina. Meanwhile, she had him over a barrel until he could somehow convince her to come about.

"Up and at 'em, Swift!" he heard her cool, melodic voice calling to him from below. It was six A.M. according to CNN, and the soft-haired siren was already starting to sing again.

Groaning, Diego hauled himself into the new pair of *blue jeans* she'd bought him the day before, along with the white *T-shirt* and work boots, and joined her in the kitchen.

"Cup of coffee?" she asked him, glancing up from the fresh fruit she was slicing.

Diego nodded wordlessly. Coffee was a luxury he'd grown used to long ago. But those *shorts* Catalina was wearing again were a sight that still left him speechless.

It was a cruel time for men to be alive when unwed women were allowed to dress in the most revealing manner imaginable and men were expected to keep their hands to themselves. But Cat had already informed him that her provocative manner of dress, with her ankles and legs almost entirely showing, wasn't the least bit shocking by twentieth-century standards. Lots of ladies wore such things. And Cat was obviously a true lady in spite of the free and easy language she used and the unshrinking way she had of doing things on her own, without asking for anyone's permission.

Bewitched, that's what all the males of this era must be if they let their women get away with it. Aye, that's what *he* was at the moment. Mesmerized by the vision of Cat with the trimmest pair of legs he'd ever seen.

And the most impudent tongue.

"How did you sleep?"

Daring, that's what it was, for a woman to come right out and ask him that. Didn't she realize what such bold talk could do to a man? "Why, naked, Catalina, same as usual."

She held the coffee cup she'd been about to sip from poised in midair. Her face took on a pink flush. "What I meant was, did you sleep well?"

Why didn't she say so in the first place? "Oh. Aye. For a man who hasn't been invited to share his own bedroom, that is."

Catalina glanced up at him with cool, unflinching composure, the copper flecks flashing in defiance. "Not in your wildest dreams, Captain. Which must be pretty good ones, considering the extent of your imagination."

Diego grinned back in amusement. What outrageous thing would the wench say next? Compared to most of the females in his past, Catalina had nerves of cast iron. She didn't pretend to be shocked by his bold brand of lovemaking. She simply fired the next blast from her cannon right back at him.

It would take a man of considerable strength and will to seduce a woman like that. A man like himself, for instance.

"Dreams can be as real as you wish to make them, *cara*. Shall I show you what I've been imagining all morning?"

"Skulls and crossbones?" Cat inquired sweetly.

"Fencing," he said, lifting the long cutlery blade from the spot on the counter where she'd laid it. "It's time you had your first lesson."

Cat swallowed hard, holding her breath as the finely honed cutting edge came toward her, moving down, down past her throat, across the shadowy dip between her breasts, hesitating finally at the uppermost button of her blouse. Her heart leapt to her throat, not from fear, but from the searing look in Diego Swift's eyes. No, it definitely wasn't fright that had sent her pulse rocketing.

It was excitement.

She knew instinctively that he wasn't going to hurt her. But there was no telling what the reckless man was going to do next. Backing slowly toward the refrigerator door, Cat wasn't sure she wanted to find out.

Diego met her movement for movement, edging forward with surprising grace and ease for a man of his size, keeping the blade perfectly poised all the while. Cat shivered as her skin made contact with the cool surface of the icebox through the thin material of her blouse. There was no room left to run.

"Lesson number one," he said. "Never let yourself be cornered. It gives the enemy the opportunity to take advantage of you."

"Advantage?" Cat repeated, hoping her voice didn't sound half as shaky as she felt.

His dark eyelashes flickered, and his shameless smile emerged. "Aye. At this point, *cara*, I could kiss you to my heart's content, and there wouldn't be a single thing you could do about it."

Cat's eyes narrowed. "You wouldn't *dare*."

His voice was soft and raspy as he leaned forward to whisper in her ear. "Wouldn't I, sweet?"

"One step closer," Cat warned dangerously, "and I'll—I'll . . ."

"Feed my insides to the alligators?" he asked, amusement in his tone.

Cat lifted her chin a notch, striving for straight-faced sarcasm. "How about your *outsides*?"

A grin flashed, sexy, irresistible. "Lesson number two, Catalina. If you are cornered—bluff. But I can see you already know that one by heart. Which leads us to lesson number three . . ."

"I *hope* it has something to do with murdering marauding pirates," she breathed fervently.

"Sorry, lass," he said, shaking his head at her, the long, dark hair falling in casual, careless waves all the way to his shoulders. "Nothing so bloodthirsty. This one is in regard to souvenirs. I always like to take a little something from my captives to remember them by."

"A little—something?"

"Aye, a memento, so to speak. And in your case, sweet, I know just what it's to be. I've taken quite a fancy to these lovely pearl buttons on your blouse."

Cat glanced down at the spherical white buttons in question. Diego wasn't the only one who'd grown attached to them. She had a certain fondness for the little fasteners herself. They were the only thing holding her shirt together!

"Get real, Swift. I'm not about to—"

But the speed and skill with which he moved was so sudden, the deed was half done before her words were out. The blade sliced, the threads gave way, and one by one the shiny round pearls dropped into his open hand.

Cat felt the the front of her blouse whisper open, revealing smooth skin, creamy white mounds, and a silky scrap of a bra that left Diego Swift struggling for air. His eyes darkened to glimmering azure, studying the view that his handiwork had revealed. For a second, the sight left him speechless.

Number four, Cat thought silently, deciding that the cocksure captain could stand to learn a lesson or two of his won. *Whenever possible, take the enemy by surprise.*

She saw the opportunity to catch him off guard. She took it.

"You do have amazing dexterity," she admitted, twisting gracefully out of his reach, "but from now on, I suggest you put it to better use."

Diego found himself inclined to agree with her suggestion. In fact, he could think of any number of ways to use his hands right now, and none of them had a thing to do with fencing.

"With a hammer and nail, for instance," she continued, cocking her chin at him. "The preservation league is meeting here in three days, and I need to get the house whipped into some semblance of shape before they show up. The front porch needs fixing, these cabinets are sagging, and the railing along the widow's walk needs reinforcing for safety's sake. That ought to keep you out of trouble for ten minutes or so, don't you think?"

The only thing Diego was inclined to think of at the moment was the very interesting undergarment Catalina had on under her blouse. What the devil was it, anyway?

"Woman," he said hoarsely, staring down at the slinky bit of silk in open curiosity, "what has become of your corset?"

She wrinkled her forehead at him, puzzled. "My—Oh!" she exclaimed, quickly catching on as she followed the direction of his glance. "Are you talking about my bra?"

"Aye," Diego agreed reverently, "if that is your word for it."

Catalina slowly shook her head at him. "And I suppose you expect me to believe you've never seen one before? But of course you haven't," she added sarcastically. "Since you claim to come from the early 1800s. The modern bra was patented in 1914, but only came into common use around the early 1940s. So you wouldn't have laid eyes on one, would you?"

"I swear I have not, sweet. It is hardly the type of thing a man would easily forget."

"Right," she responded doubtfully. "Then you better get a good look at this one, Captain, because it's the last you're going to see of it." And with that outspoken pronouncement, she peeled the rest of the blouse clear away.

Diego began to realize he was in the presence of an opponent more formidable than he'd first imagined. A female with more raw nerve than any scoundrel he'd ever met. And a surplus of brains to boot. For the first time in his life, he felt himself to be evenly matched.

"That, Catalina," he said slowly, "would be an insufferable shame. But I will do my best to observe it carefully, just in case."

With a sigh of exasperation, she disappeared into the next room, presumably for a fresh garment. Smiling, Diego shoved the handful of pearls into the front pocket of his blue jeans. He was beginning to like this new century he found himself in.

Cat couldn't sleep. In spite of all the hard work she and Diego had put in over the past few days, the house was far from the shape she'd wanted it to be in for the beautification board. The meeting she'd scheduled with them was only two days away, but instead of catching up on the rest of the improvements she needed to finish before the deadline, she was lying there worrying about how she was going to get it all done.

Sighing, she switched on her bedside lamp, then leaned back against her headboard, eyeing the bedroom walls in disgust. Or, more precisely, the wallpaper. It had probably been applied sometime in the fifties, and was definitely the most putrid shade of flocked green she'd ever seen. She had been itching to strip it off since the first day she'd seen it, but other matters in the house had taken priority. Now, she wasn't sure if she could live with it a moment longer.

It certainly had to go before the board showed up. She could only imagine the raised eyebrows and upturned noses that twelve-foot-high fuzzy walls would invite. Of course, Cat had every intention of returning the surface to its original, simply painted plaster, but the biddies on the board might not have enough imagination to see past its current, hideous state.

Throwing back the covers, Cat padded barefoot across the cool expanse of coquina floor, heading for the wooden stepladder that was stowed inside her closet. So what if it was past midnight? If she couldn't sleep, she might as well put her energy to good use.

Dragging the ladder out and unfolding it into position, she had just made her way up the first three rungs when there was a sudden, insistent pounding at her bedroom door. Diego. Oh, dear, she'd probably woken him up with all the racket.

"Come in," she called, still balancing herself on the middle step.

The door flew open. Diego entered, wearing nothing but the boxer shorts she'd bought him several days ago. The long black mass of his hair fell in sexy, sleep-tousled waves across his strongly tanned shoulders, and the brilliant blue of his eyes stared at her in stern reproof.

"What the devil are you doing up at his hour,

Catalina?" he asked her in a voice that was clearly accustomed to the authority of command.

"Stripping wallpaper," she explained calmly. "Go back to bed, Captain. I'm sorry I woke you."

"I care naught for that," he told her, his voice softening slightly, "but it's late, lass, and you've already put in a long day's work. Surely the wallpaper will wait until morning."

"Probably," she admitted, "but I won't. I couldn't sleep. Let's just call the work a cure for insomnia and leave it at that."

But instead of leaving, Diego boldly settled himself on the edge of her bed and folded his arms across his chest, studying her. "Is this house so important to you, lass, that you would slave away all night for the sake of it?"

Catalina hesitated. "Yes," she finally told him, a little surprised at the truth of it herself. "It's a bit hard to explain, but I was looking for more than just a house when I bought the place. This is the closest I've ever come to having a real home."

Now what had made her admit that to him? Sleep deprivation, no doubt. Or maybe it was the look of understanding that she read in his expression. Maybe she wasn't the only one who was lacking roots in her life. Diego appeared to be pretty much adrift himself. A wanderer.

But in his case, the freewheeling spirit seemed to be one of conscious choice. One look in those reckless eyes and it was obvious that the man was born for adventure. He was content to go where the wind blew him.

"I guess that may be hard for you to understand," Cat added, seating herself on the ladder rung as she met his gaze across the room, "the fact that I want something in my life that feels stable and secure. You strike me as a guy who prefers to live more on the edge, am I right? I wonder if you've ever stayed in the same place for more than a month or two at a time."

"No need to wonder," he said, flashing her a wide white grin. "I have not. I did not build my house at the edge of the ocean simply to admire the view. In fact, I never did dock here for long. I saw no reason to."

"I see," Cat responded, shaking her head. Whether or not Diego believed he had owned this house at one time, he still looked at the world through very different eyes. "That's what life is to you, isn't it?" she asked him. "Just one long adventure."

"Aye," he agreed heartily. "One great adventure, and landing in this new century the grandest of them all. Who would have thought that I might live to see so many modern miracles? Why settle down, lass, when something even more amazing may be waiting for you just over the next wave?"

"Simple," she said. "Because no matter how far you go, there's nothing out there that's better than home."

"It is an appealing thought, sweet, but a building

does not welcome one home with open arms. It takes a warm and willing body to do that."

Exactly how, Cat wondered, had the conversation taken such a dangerous turn? Warm and willing bodies? It occurred to her that having a close, intimate conversation with a man like Swift in her bedroom so late at night might not be a good idea. It might give him the wrong impression, she realized.

Or the right one.

Climbing down off the ladder, she headed for the doorway and the comforting safety of the overhead light switch.

"What is it, lass?" he asked softly, checking her forward progress with a steadying hand at the hem of her nightgown. "Have I said something to disturb you?"

Catalina froze in place, her heart firing up to full speed. Once again, she was beginning to lose control of the situation with Diego. What was it about this particular man that made her feel that way? As if she was about to lose control of herself.

There was no telling what would happen at this point if she was foolish enough to show him any weakness. "Of course not," she insisted. "Nothing you could do would disturb me."

But Diego didn't believe her. Instead of releasing her, he called her bluff. "Indeed? Are you sure about that, sweet?"

"One-hundred-percent sure," she shot back boldly.

"Throwing down the gauntlet, Catalina?" he asked in amusement, grabbing her securely by the wrist and pulling her down on the bed beside him. "Don't you realize that a challenge like that is impossible for any red-blooded pirate to resist?"

FOUR

In one quick, heart-stopping moment, Cat found herself flat on her back beneath Diego Swift, her body sinking into the softness of the mattress as he pinned her arms helplessly over her head. Her wrists were locked in the implacable grip of one powerful hand as he tentatively touched her face with the other, testing the softness of her skin with the work-roughened surface of his fingertips.

The sensation was one of the most sensual Cat had ever known. The tactile contrast of coarse against smooth, of callused male skin against tender female flesh. His touch was slow, exploratory, surprisingly gentle for a man of his size and strength.

Surprisingly seductive. He was only touching her *face* for heaven's sake, but the gesture was far from innocent. A lover's touch, that's what it was. A stroking that left her stomach weak, her heart pounding wildly, and the rest of her wanting . . .

More.

The lamplight shone in the depths of his eyes, revealing the single, overwhelming emotion that was written there. Desire.

Cat came close to drowning in those baby blues. She felt paralyzed by the power of his sensual surveillance, as if, somehow, his searing glance could probe her private, most intimate thoughts. In seconds, he'd penetrated every last one of her defenses and taken possession of her mind. And now he seemed set on doing the same with her body.

His mouth drew close, nearly touching hers, so close, Catalina's lips parted in anticipation. An involuntary reaction on her part, she assured herself, no more than a reflex response. But the captain clearly didn't agree.

"Curious, Catalina?" he asked, so near, she felt his breath brushing over her, teasing her with heat and hoarseness, with a warm, musky maleness that threatened to turn her insides to mush. "Wondering what it would be like to kiss a genuine swashbuckler, are you?"

"I'd sooner kiss a stingray," she shot back smoothly, amazed that she was able to speak at all under the circumstances.

The feel of his body flush up against hers was making it hard to breathe. Not from the massively muscled weight of him, which would've squashed her like a bug by now if he hadn't known just how to hold himself, but from the way that weight was distributed. The bare heat of his thighs, sinking into hers, the pressure of his hips, melding with her own, the rigid evidence of his arousal, granite-hard, pressing bluntly at the narrow cleft between her legs.

"Would you now, lass?" he asked, his voice rife with amusement. "And I suppose you'd rather sleep with a slimy squid than bed down with an unscrupulous sea-wolf like me?"

"You catch on quick, Captain."

"Making love with a moray eel, would, in fact, be preferable?"

"Far more pleasant," she agreed.

A quick, cocky grin flashed. Apparently Diego was enjoying himself. Damn him, but he knew she was lying!

"Such defiance, Catalina," he said. "Such rebellious resistance. Were we on my ship, I would have to boot you overboard for insulting the captain so. But since we are in my bed—"

"*Your* bed?" she breathed.

"Aye. My bed, *cara*. But I have no inclination to boot you out of it. I wonder what your punishment should be instead?"

"Fifty lashes, no doubt," she murmured sarcastically.

"You wound me to the quick, Catalina. What sort of dog do you take me for? Only the lowest sort of man would lay whip to a woman."

"I wasn't serious! But it's a relief to hear you have *some* scruples, after all."

"Aye," he acknowledged with a lazy smile, "but not enough to save you. Nay, lass, I can think of only one fitting way to silence your cruel insults. A sheer torture indeed for a wench who'd rather touch fish lips than my own."

"Torture?" Cat squeaked.

"A long and slow one," the captain promised sternly.

No, she meant to say. But as she parted her lips to tell him so, the heat of his mouth enveloped her and his tongue stole recklessly inside.

Cat was conquered in a matter of seconds. All thoughts of protest were effectively silenced by the sweet shock of sensation flowing through her. Hopelessly lost in the kiss from the instant his mouth touched hers, she gave herself over to the punishing, sinful pleasure of it.

It was hot and daring, probing so deeply that every rhythmic stroke he delivered demanded nothing less than her total surrender. A plundering kiss, a ravaging act of sheer, sexual torture designed to strip her senseless.

And doing a darn good job of it.

She moaned softly as Diego repeatedly plumbed the open warmth of her with his tongue, infusing himself inside her until her stomach muscles clenched in excitement. Gracious, she thought feverishly, stunned by what he was doing to her. Stunned by the fact that she was allowing it!

No decent woman would permit a man like Swift—a stranger, really—to seduce her so boldly in her own bedroom. But then, Cat had never been a hundred percent sure whether or not she really was decent. The captain, she knew, definitely was not!

But neither was he the demented psycho she'd first figured him for. This was no trench-coat-toting exhibitionist she was dealing with here. Diego Swift would never settle for a quick flash-and-dash. He wanted to *participate*.

In fact, he seemed to know ways to pleasure a woman that Cat, in her very limited experience with men, had never even imagined. Secret touches, words whispered against her mouth that sent urgent thrills spiraling through her. He was speaking to her in fluent Spanish, she realized, but the vocabulary was nothing she'd ever heard in Sister Mary Margaret's foreign language class. His accent was perfect, and if the exact translation was somewhat hazy, the general meaning was quickly clear to Cat.

Pillow talk was what it was, the kind of sexy, illicit language that could only be whispered in the bedroom. There was a cosmopolitan quality about it that surprised her, a rough sophistication in his low, throaty tone that was worldly and seductive at the same time. The sound of his voice left her weak. The fluency of it made her wonder.

Where had he ever learned to speak such elegant, albeit uncensored Spanish?

"*Cara*," he said, his breath hot in her ear.

Cara? That meant dear, didn't it? It was a little hard to remember at the moment, but in her effort to recall, the formidable Sister Mary Margaret's face flashed suddenly before her.

If there was ever an image that could make a schoolgirl shudder, it was the sight of that forbidding teacher, her long, bony finger shaking a stern accusation. The memory of it worked on Cat as effectively as a cold shower. Heaven help her, but she was behaving every bit as brazenly as the sister had always predicted.

She had to stop herself, now, before the pure physical power of what they were doing swept all sense of reason away. Gratification, she reminded herself, was no acceptable substitute for good sense. With the sister's harsh warning still echoing in her ears, she sat up in bed, shivering.

Thankfully, Diego made no attempt to stop her. He rolled over onto his back and let out a low, frustrated groan. "What is it, lass?" he demanded, not unkindly. "A ghost walking across your grave?"

Deserting the bed for safety's sake, Catalina crossed to the window and stared out at the big black ocean beyond. "Something like that," she explained, letting the soft breeze blow over her. "Only more like a cold blast from my past. I was back at school for a minute there, remembering a nun I once knew . . ."

Diego shook his head slowly, wondering if seawater had somehow lodged between his ears. He could hardly credit what he was hearing. He had kissed Catalina with everything he had, a magnificent, maiden-melting kiss if he said so himself. But instead of contemplating the mad, passionate love he was making to her, she was thinking about *nuns*? Was

Diablo Swift losing his touch or was this particular woman more challenging than most?

"Come back here, *cara*," he enticed, propping himself up on one elbow and giving the mattress a suggestive thump, "and I will smite that obstinate nun from your mind. Perhaps my passion was too tame for you the first time. A second kiss from me will send that sister fleeing, I swear."

"Too tame?" she asked, turning back toward him, eyes wide. "No, it wasn't that. It's me. I—I'm not very good at this sort of thing."

Was the vixen teasing him, Diego wondered? She was so gifted at the *sort of thing* they'd just done, it made him ache. Never had a woman responded so sweetly and honestly to his advances. There had been no playacting on her part, no contriving or calculating designed to entangle him in some convoluted female snare. This woman had wanted him for himself, nothing more.

Almost as much as he wanted her now.

"Lass," he said hoarsely, "surely you jest."

"Don't you see?" she asked him, her voice soft and tense. "I *can't* be good at it. It's not very nineties of me, I know, but that's the way I was raised at the convent."

"A convent, Catalina? Never say you were studying to take the vows." A terrible waste that would be, he decided, a crying shame for a lady of Ms. Steadwell's obvious talents to be called to a life of celibacy. Just the thought of it was enough to make the angels weep.

She shook her head, laughing lightly. "I thought about it," she explained, "but catechism was never my best subject. History was always so fascinating. Besides, the nuns didn't think I was suited for a life of grace, considering my background. My parents were hippies," she added, attempting to enlighten him.

"Hippies?" he repeated, frowning. "Were they loyalist descendants of the British invasion?"

"Not unless you're referring to the Beatles," she responded dryly. "My folks were more into tie-dye, shag rugs, lava lamps, that sort of stuff. And the biggest revolution they took part in was the sexual one. Don't tell me you've never heard of *that*."

A revolution fought for sexual reasons? Diego was regretful he'd missed it. Unlike the land-grabbing, culture-marauding causes of his time, that sounded like an issue that would've been worth fighting for. "Sorry, lass," he said, "but that battle, too, has completely passed me by. Would you be so good as to tell me who won?"

Her eyebrows arched in surprise, as if the question was one she'd never considered before. "Who won?" she repeated, hesitating. "I'm afraid the jury's still out on that one. But personally, I think the misfit children of that generation were the ones who lost. The children who weren't sure where they belonged. My parents wanted physical love without any of the responsibility or legal commitment of marriage. Which might've worked out just fine if they hadn't brought a child into the world as a result."

Catalina grimaced. "I know my folks never expected to die so suddenly," she confided, "but if they had been married at the time, at least the sisters and the students at school might not have treated me like some shameful mistake."

Diego felt a rift of anger rip through him, as intense as it was unexpected. He had a sudden urge to throttle a bunch of overzealous nuns with his bare hands, an act that would no doubt seal the coffin on his ultimate fate. A voyage straight to hell in a handbasket. But he'd been heading in that general direction for some time now, and at least he would go down fighting for something. Fighting for Catalina, anyway. Odd, but the one woman who was spirited enough to wage her own battles was the only one who'd ever roused this streak of chivalry in him.

"How is it possible, Catalina," he demanded fiercely, "that in this modern world, a child of love could still be regarded as a mistake?"

Moonlight streamed in on her through the windowpane, bathing her hair, her hands, her body with an unearthly, ethereal glow. Diego felt himself in the presence of an angel from another world, another time. An angel sent to save him or punish him, he wasn't sure which.

She shrugged, having no answer for him, but a grateful smile softened her pale features.

He kicked back against the bed, raking the hair from his eyes, determined not to miss a moment of this fine, twentieth-century scenery. "Had I been born of love like you, lass, I might never have turned to piracy. But I was sired as an act of need, instead, in a West Indies brothel by a man who never cared to know my mother's name."

Catalina let out a soft gasp of surprise. "Your mother was a . . . ?"

"Saint," he finished firmly. "Her lot in life was hard. Selling her body was the only way she knew to make a living. But when my father came along one night, a wealthy seafaring merchant, he promised her great riches in return for his pleasure. And left without paying a single peso. That's what my mother remembered about him the most," he added bitterly. "He had refused to pay."

"I'm—sorry," Catalina whispered.

"Aye," Diego agreed coldly, "and so was he. The sorriest bastard that ever lived once I was through with him. His cargo-laden trading ships were the first I ever went after. Easy targets, they were. He paid for that night in the end, with the only thing that mattered to him. His fortune. The bloody scavenger, I *made* him pay."

Cat felt the goose bumps starting to break out along her arms. As incredible as Diego's story sounded, the force of his feelings was obviously real. Strong enough, in fact, to pull sharply on her own heartstrings. He believed what he was saying. *He was beginning to make her believe in it too.*

Was she losing her mind along with him, she wondered, caught up in the sheer, overwhelming charisma of the man? Or was there actually some shred of credibility in the clear confidence of his words? One thing was certain, he knew too much to simply be inventing the details as he went along. The smooth-spoken Spanish, for instance, roughened by a hint of hot and racy island dialect. The fencing maneuvers, lightning-fast enough to lop off the extremities of any opponent so foolish as to cross his path.

The way he'd kissed her.

Passionately. Possessively. With all the arrogance of a man who didn't know it was his modern, civilized duty to *ask* a woman first, make calm, consensual love to her later.

She studied him from across the room, admitting secretly that Diego Swift certainly *looked* the part of a pirate. Now more than ever, with his dark hair swept back in wild disarray against his bare shoulders, and a dangerous don't-mess-with-me look in his blazing eyes.

A look of anger for the father who'd hurt him, Cat reminded herself. Maybe for every careless, greedy enemy he'd encountered since. Were they the personal demons he'd been chasing all of his life or the one's he'd been running from when he'd wound up on her floor?

"I *want* to believe you," she admitted to him now.

"I've never lied to you, lass," he promised softly. "Except maybe about liking these clothes you try to crowd me into," he added, flashing her a sudden white smile. "These *boxer shorts* are scratching at my skin."

"I'm sure you'll get used to them," she murmured, feeling her face growing warm again.

The fit of Diego's underwear wasn't a subject she felt strong enough to discuss at the moment. At least not while he was lying on her bed, stretched out like he belonged there, barefoot and sleep-rumpled and grinning wickedly.

"Nay," he told her firmly, "never. I can see no use for the infernal contraptions. Just *look* at the bloody things, lass. They are slack as mainsails becalmed by the breeze. Where is all this material to go when I am wearing breeches? There is no room for it, sweet, I assure you. And they are so poorly sewn as to have a large opening right here in the front, where none should be. A little starch in my shorts, so to speak, one wrong move, and there may be all manner of unexpected consequences. You would not imagine them to be so fine if a surprise such as that should take place."

Cat's face was burning wildly by now, her whole body hot with excruciating embarrassment. Did the captain have no sense of modesty where his body was concerned? Apparently not, she decided, but then, why should he when it was so perfect?

She directed her eyes heavenward, attempting to calm her thoughts, not to mention her hammering heart. Just the idea of discussing Diego's anatomy was enough to make her breath catch sharply in her throat. The conversation reminded her all too vividly of the view she'd had of him from the rear, a sight that no living, feeling woman could ever forget.

One eyeful from that direction and the word *well-built* seemed woefully inadequate. Shockingly virile, that's what the captain was. Way too much man for someone like her. Too potent, too male, too *macho*.

As for the boxer shorts, and the full frontal view that still lay hidden inside—Cat would just as soon keep it that way. She didn't even want to *think* about what an image like that might do to her. Swift was a big boy, she decided. A *very* big boy. And he would just have to manage his skivvies himself.

"I really don't care if you wear any at all!" she insisted.

His dark eyebrows lifted skeptically. "Indeed, sweet? Then I assure you I won't."

"Fine then," she told him. "All right. Okay."

"Okay, Catalina."

"Time for bed," she suggested.

"I'm in bed, lass."

"Upstairs!" she clarified. "In your cot. I think we've both had enough excitement for one night."

"Speak for yourself, *cara*," he said, rising to leave. "Speak for yourself."

Cat pored over the stack of paperwork on her desk, trying her best to concentrate on the reams of dry historical data. Population statistics of the Victorian era. A report on the rate of industrial growth in the post–Civil War period. Normally, it was an easy task to skim the information and catalog it for the historical society's overflowing information files. But the intellectual focus she'd learned to count on over the years had lately begun to elude her.

It just wasn't easy to keep your mind on work when there was a man like Swift waiting for you at home. A pirate in the house. It was proving to be a serious distraction.

Sighing, she leaned back in her rickety office chair and pushed the reports away. She wasn't much use to anyone in her current, distracted condition, least of all the society's meticulously maintained library. At the rate she was going, the 1850s' population would end up somewhere in the Flagler era, a risqué period of prohibition and partying that the prim Victorians would hardly appreciate. Not to mention the folks who relied on the library for research.

Research, she repeated silently as a thought struck her. What if she were to conduct a little private research of her own, just out of curiosity? What better place to start than the basement of the very building she was in, where data was stored dating back to Pedro Menéndez de Avilés, the first European to establish a local community?

Was it possible there were records of later seafaring activities somewhere down in that basement as well? Records of the old ports, for instance, of the St. Augustine Inlet and Salt Run, of the Matanzas Waterway, the Intracoastal and the men who'd once sailed them. Were there any clear, recorded facts left behind of the pirates that had passed this way?

Pushing back from her desk, Cat decided there

was only one way to find out. In minutes, she'd descended to the bottom floor and let herself inside the musty, low-ceilinged room. The smell of old books assailed her, sweet and dusty.

Two hours later her hands were dry from the parchment she'd been handling, her stocking-covered knees were dirty from kneeling beside the stacks, and several wayward strands of hair had escaped from the confinement of her prim, businesslike bun. But Cat didn't care. She'd found what she was looking for.

The page was cream and crisp, brittle with age, the india ink slightly faded, but still legible after all this time. The account of it was all there, in flowing black and white. A mention of a ship going down in rough weather, in the month of August, year 1810.

A ship called the *Mystress*, said to have foundered some miles off the coast after a harrowing encounter with a strange and sudden hurricane. The crew had been found several days later, thirsty but safe in their lifeboats. Only two men were believed to have drowned, although their bodies were never recovered. The first mate, for one, by the name of Mister Scurvy. And the captain himself, an infamous pirate, ruffian, and generally dangerous character by all accounts.

Captain Diego Swift.

FIVE

By the time she'd finished reading, Cat's heart was in her throat and a sense of detached reality was beginning to take hold of her, sending slow, uneasy shivers along her spine. It was true, all of it. Everything he'd told her.

No, she decided desperately, it was *worse* than true. There were parts of Swift's remarkable story he'd never seen fit to tell her. *And no wonder.*

Diablo Swift, the historical account called him. The devil. A daring, unscrupulous, rapscallion of a privateer. A scoundrel and a rogue who had believed the world was his oyster, with treasure and women mere pearls for the taking.

He was *real*, heaven help her. He was alive and well, in the twentieth century, having somehow been swept forward in time. *He was in her house at this very moment.*

Oh Lord, Cat wondered, just what sort of man

had she allowed to sleep under her roof these past two weeks? Correction, *their* roof. For all she knew, her beloved house might legally still belong to him. She couldn't kick him out of it now.

She didn't dare.

Oh hell, she wasn't even sure she wanted to!

How had it happened? How had Swift, a pirate from the distant past, wound up wet and naked on her floor? He had been shipwrecked, that much was clear. He'd made it to shore and headed for home.

And then she had found him, passed out from fatigue. But that still didn't explain the most mysterious part of his journey. It didn't explain what strange forces had been at work that night, forces powerful enough to propel a man almost two hundred years into the future.

It occurred to Cat that the information she'd just discovered was less than perfect proof of Swift's true identity. Diego whoever-he-is might have read the same story and decided to scam her with it in some way. But deep in her gut, she knew it wasn't so.

Her house, the only thing she owned of any real value, wasn't even worth a con man's effort. And if some low-crawling sleazoid had wanted to cheat her out of it, he would surely have come up with a more believable story! Shipwrecks and swashbucklers were the stuff that fairy tales were made of, not the sort of solid, reliable facts that a confidence man would use to inspire . . . confidence.

No, she believed Swift, heaven help her, from the

bottom of her heart. She just didn't understand exactly how this historical mix-up had occurred.

Theoretically, she knew such a thing was possible. At least it was according to her old physics professor and some very complex space-time calculations that Einstein had once made. But Cat had excelled at history, not science, and she was still at a loss about how to explain it.

She could only guess that the very weird weather front Diego's ship had sailed into had something to do with it. The crew's account of the storm certainly made it sound out of the ordinary. According to them, the first mate and the captain had been sucked into a black, whirling vortex that the hurricane had spun off, and were never seen again. Was it possible that the cyclone they described was more than a mere tornado touching down?

Had Swift somehow been pulled into a funnel of black space powerful enough to punch through the fabric of time itself? The phenomenon's tunnel shape must have drawn him in at one century and dumped him out in another.

Dumped him out *here*.

Cat wasn't sure she could come to terms with it all. She only understood that the problem Diego posed was immediate. Now that she knew where he'd come from and when, the question still remained: What was she going to do about him?

Pirate or not, Diego had come in pretty handy around the old place so far. He seemed to have a knack for making all the rusty, run-down gadgets run smoothly. The attic window latch. The squeaking floorboards. The lock on her bedroom door.

Her bedroom, Cat thought, swallowing hard, remembering all too vividly the way he'd kissed her there. It was his bedroom, too, based on what she'd just learned.

His *bed*.

She'd been fantasizing about that night ever since. Yes, *fantasizing*—she had to admit it. But just what sort of rakish character had she been living with anyway?

And just how many other women had been swept away by his considerable charms in that exact same spot? Dozens and dozens, no doubt, if the tales they told of him were true. Women far more experienced than she.

Luckily, *she* had learned of his reputation in time. And if Swift imagined that she was still in danger of succumbing to his irresistible animal magnetism, he would soon learn a thing or two about what modern women were made of. Tough stuff. They could get along just fine *without* a man in their life, thank you.

At least, Catalina Steadwell could. She'd survived thus far without one, hadn't she? Sure, Swift had helped her out quite a bit with the restorations, but that was what she was paying him for, wasn't it? Services rendered, *not* stud service.

Of course, he did make her feel much safer in her bed at night, she admitted, softening toward him slightly. Yes, she was safe with a man like that in the house, she decided. From everyone but him!

She could hardly wait to confront him. Making a photocopy of all the juicy details she'd just found, she carefully tucked the papers in her suit pocket and headed home to do just that.

The meeting didn't go at all the way she'd imagined.

"So, *Diablo*," she began, "what do you have to say for yourself?"

He was wearing Walt's overalls again, she realized, with the bib down and his broad, paganesque torso bare to the waist, giving him a decidedly unfair advantage. He'd been painting this morning, apparently, and there were cream-white flecks spattered in the coarse, dark matt of his chest hair and scattered across the proud bridge of his nose. Boyish and cocky, that's how he looked. And incredibly pleased with himself, especially after reading the paper she'd handed him.

At least he could read, Cat acknowledged, which was something of an accomplishment for a scoundrel of his century. The man had so *many* talents.

"Well, Conan?" she prompted impatiently.

"Catalina!" he exclaimed, almost crowing with pleasure, "this is good news, indeed. Very good news, lass, to hear that my crew made it out of that storm alive."

His crew? Cat hadn't really considered that angle of the story. It had all seemed to happen so long ago, with the outcome reading like just another line in the pages of history. But to Diego, the incident had been recent, and the men in those lifeboats were real. He had cared about them, she realized. Cared a lot, if his enthusiastic reaction was anything to go by.

Her hostility began to ebb just a little. A captain who took the safety of his crew to heart couldn't be *all* bad, could he? But then, it wasn't his dealings with his men she'd been concerned about. It was his reputation with women that worried her!

"All except Scurvy," he added, disheartened. "Stubborn old man. You would've enjoyed his company, Catalina. Aye, the pair of you have so much in common."

"Am I supposed to take that as a compliment?" she demanded.

"Naturally, *cara*. I am likening you to the gritty man who was once my closest friend."

"Well," Cat responded dryly, "at least I can't accuse you of trying to sweet-talk your way out of this."

"Sweet-talk, Catalina?" he asked, crowding her up against the kitchen wall, planting his arms on either side of her shoulders in a position that could only be described as predatory, making it virtually impossible for her to move. "Is that what you're after?"

Cat stared up into his electric, blue eyes, determined not to be affected by them this time. Bandit eyes, she thought, her throat going dry. The kind that could pierce a a woman's soul with a single glance and steal her heart with a wink.

"No!" she insisted, carefully directing her own gaze to a blank stretch of space just to the left of the captain's shoulder. "I think you owe me some sort of explanation."

"I owe you more than that, *cara*," he said, taking her chin in his hand and coaxing her face back toward him. "You took me in, gave me food, shelter, *blue jeans*. Why will you not let me thank you properly and give you pleasure in return?"

"Maybe because I'd rather not be just another notch on your sword hilt, *Diablo*," she said, patting herself mentally on the back for how casual she sounded. It wasn't easy to keep your cool when a man like Swift had you in his sights. She was hip to hip with a real pirate, for mercy's sake!

His eyelids narrowed in understanding, his eyelashes dark and thick against the sun-crinkled skin. "Ah, sweet, I see. It is my roving past that has you so upset. Need I remind you that the deeds described in that history account took place nearly two hundred years ago, long before we met?"

Cat eyed him squarely, summoning her strength. She wanted to know facts, details, anything that would back up what the logical half of her brain had believed all along. The captain was trouble on two feet. A heartache in overalls. Bad news for good girls, no matter what century he was in.

"It's true then?" she asked. "You were that dangerous character they wrote about, with a woman in every port?"

The dark eyebrows rose as he considered the

question at length. "Nay, lass," he finally admitted, "not exactly. It's a fact I made off with a fortune in coin, but I never sank another ship in the process, or killed a man unless it was in self-defense. As for ravishing unwilling wenches wherever I went"—a smile flashed at the recollection—"I can assure you that all were willing. But the account *is* something of an exaggeration."

"So you had a woman in every *other* port, then," she corrected. "That makes me feel *so* much better."

He released her, raking the long hair back from his forehead, folding his arms across his wide, wide chest in restrained frustration. "What would you have me say, Catalina? I am a man, not a saint. There are deeds in my past I am not proud of, but I am nearing forty now, and it is too late to undo them. Fate has seen fit to punish me for my crimes, else why would I have lost everything except my life?"

Compassion welled in Cat at his words. Was it possible that what had happened to him really was some sort of divine, cosmic fate, designed to make him see the error of his plundering ways? Or had he been sent here for some other reason? An answer to a prayer, for instance. The silent, secret kind that women whispered into their pillows at night.

Other women, Cat reassured herself. Not her.

"I don't know why this has happened," she told him, "or how. But there are some semirational scientific theories that might explain it. Although the idea of an avenging angel of justice makes just as much sense, considering your criminal past."

"I once thought I was that avenging angel," he said. "But the heavens have struck me down for my insolence. Redemption is what I require now, Catalina. Can you not find it in your heart to forgive the angry young ne'er-do-well I once was?"

She had a compelling urge to touch him, forgive him anything, surrender her guard. The realization terrified her almost as much as the man himself. What if she did surrender to Diego Swift? He wasn't the type to take prisoners.

He would take all of her.

Much more than she could afford to risk. In fact, Swift was starting to make her feel things no good Catholic girl should ever dream about. Racy, erotic, downright *sinful* things.

But as attracted as she was to this man, nothing was going to happen between them. Nothing more, anyway. She wouldn't let it.

The captain just wasn't the sort who would ever settle down and give her the "piece of paper" that experience had taught her was so important. He was a wanderer by nature, a man with no roots. He'd been born in a brothel, for heaven's sake, and raised to believe that men and women were meant to *make* love, not *fall* in love and get married.

Whoever had heard of a married pirate, anyway?

And he certainly hadn't earned that revealing nickname by staying with the same woman for long. Or in the same place for that matter. Sooner or later, when he finally adjusted to this new century, Cat knew he would be sailing off again.

Without her.

"It's not my place to forgive you," she told him finally. "But there are a few things you need to understand about twentieth-century women."

"Indeed?" he asked her.

"First of all," she said, "we're not *wenches*."

"Aye," he agreed, nodding. "This is something I have learned from *cable television*. Now you are *babes*."

"What have you been watching?" Cat inquired sweetly. "Beer commercials?"

"Nay," he corrected her. "ESPN. *The station for real sports.*"

"Uh-huh. Well, here's another thing, Swift. No more physical contact unless you *ask* me first. No touching. No swooping down on a person when she isn't prepared for it. No—kissing."

"You don't like kissing, Catalina?"

"That's not the point! It's just not done nowadays unless both people have agreed to it in advance. In fact, *nothing* is done between male and female adults anymore without a great deal of discussion beforehand. It's more controlled that way. More civilized."

"Civilized?" he repeated, lifting a skeptical eyebrow at her. "With social mores such as that, sweet, it is a miracle any people remain to populate this modern civilization of yours."

"I didn't make the rules," she protested.

"Nay, but you wish me to follow them. Forgive me, *cara*, but now I see how it is that a woman such as you can remain *unhitched* at the advanced age of twenty-nine. The men of this day know not how to make love!"

"Advanced age?" Cat seethed. "You're not exactly a spring chicken yourself, Swift! And by the way, have *you* ever been married?"

He stared at her as if the concept was completely foreign. "Leg-shackled? Are you jesting me, lass?"

"No, just making a point," she said, and walked out of the room, leaving the captain to figure it out for himself.

Tossing back and forth on his cot at two in the morning, Diego still hadn't deciphered the mystery of Ms. Catalina Steadwell, the tempting, tormenting, twentieth-century *babe*. In spite of his considerable experience with the opposite sex, he was all at sea when it came to handling an up-to-date *fox* like her.

Aye, she was right about one thing. The rules had changed a hell of a lot in two hundred years. So much, they'd thrown him off keel. Blasted him right out of the water, as it were.

Had *she* been sent back to his time, instead, he would have known precisely how to proceed. Sweeping her dramatically off to his ship in a fierce, romantic fashion would have been a fine way to start. Unfortunately, that option was no longer available to him.

His beautiful vessel was growing barnacles at the bottom of the ocean by now. And according to Catalina, such grand, manly gestures were no longer admired. She would probably laugh at him and tell him to "get a grip."

The most puzzling part of all was the way she'd reacted to the historical account. She finally believed him. But no sooner had she convinced herself that the tale he'd told her was true, than she desired him to reform his swashbuckling ways.

He had made no effort to conceal his identity from her, revealing, most honestly, the accurate nature of his pirate's life. In truth, Diego really didn't mind going down in the history ledgers as an infamous brigand. He had hoped the tale would make it harder for Catalina to reject his advances.

He'd been wrong. She had rejected them, even more obstinately than before.

Just who was the modern moron, Diego wanted to know, who had invented these damn fool rules of sexual etiquette?

Did Catalina truly expect him to beg for her favors over a tepid cup of tea? Nay, he would never run tame for her, no matter how near to begging he was. Pleading was no prelude to passion.

A plague upon her rules, Diego decided. Rules were meant to be broken. Aye, there was only one thing in the way of their mutual bliss. Catalina's infernal stubbornness.

She wouldn't admit she wanted him.

A self-respecting pirate would prove that to her by deed, not word. He would captivate her by the sheer force of his will, carry her off to his bedroom, and ravish her so thoroughly, there would be no time for speeches. No time for anything beyond the sound of her sighs as he pleasured her.

Clearly there was only one thing required on his part. Immediate action. He saw no reason to put it off any longer. He would strike now, while the iron, so to speak, was hot.

Five minutes later, blue jean–clad and barefoot, he was banging at her bedroom door. "Open the door for me, lass. It's locked."

"Swift," she groaned, "it's two A.M. Go to bed."

Blast it all, but that was exactly what he was trying to do. What the devil did she mean by locking him out, anyway? Was Catalina scared of him? The possibility pleased him. She would be fainting in his arms before long now.

He knocked again. "Awaken, wench, if you know what's good for you."

Promising sounds began to emanate from inside. A muttered curse, a scrambling of lovely little feet across the floor. The door flew open, and she stood before him, breathing hard.

"*Wench?* Would you like to run that past me again, Swift?"

"Nay, lass, it is you I would like. I am here to sweep you off your bare feet."

Her copper eyes widened in sleepy disbelief. "Excuse me?"

"There will be no excuses this time, *cara*. Only fulfillment."

She crossed her slim arms in front of her, stubbornly standing her ground. Aye, Diego thought, she was a worthy wench, headstrong and full of spirit. Desire lanced through him, sharp as a fencing foil. Make no mistake, he meant to have her.

"I *hope* you're referring to job fulfillment," she shot back at him. "As in having a sudden itch to hang some wallpaper that just can't wait?"

"Sorry, sweet, but wallpaper is the furthest thing from my mind right now. Prepare yourself to be ravished, because I am unwilling to put this moment off any longer."

"*Ravished*, Captain?" she asked, half laughing. "Now, really—"

But Diego was through with talking. Turning a deaf ear to her protests, he picked her up in his arms, flung her easily over his shoulder and started back up the stairs to the attic.

This couldn't be happening, Catalina thought, as he wielded her silk-clad body as smoothly and effortlessly as he might have handled a small sack of potatoes. He really meant to ravish her!

She clutched at his bare back, unsure whether to scream or to giggle hysterically. There was no one around to hear anyway, no one to save her from him. *No one around to save her from herself.*

"Diego," she protested, striving for a sense of cool, rational calm she was far from feeling. "This is crazy. You've obviously been watching too many Errol Flynn reruns on the oldies channel again."

"Hush, Catalina, or I will still your mouth with my bandanna."

"What! Just try it, sailor, and I'll, I'll . . ."

"Run me through?" he supplied, laughing heartily.

"I *wish*," she breathed hotly, bouncing along.

Cat squeezed her eyes shut again, feeling dizzy at the sight of the handrail whizzing past her, upside down. Not to mention the image of Diego's enormous back, where the muscles seemed to stretch for miles and miles, lithely rippling with every movement he made, undulating dangerously down until they finally disappeared into the narrow belt of his blue jeans. All that flexing male flesh was starting to have a strangely disturbing effect on her.

Closing her eyes, unfortunately, wasn't enough to block the erotic vision from her mind. If anything, the blind feel of him was even more powerful, the sensation of being caught bodily up against all that raw machismo nothing short of stunning. Lord help her, even the smell of him was enough to send her senses into overload.

He carried her into his makeshift bedroom and laid her down on the cot. Awareness swirled through her as he sat down beside her. The strap of her nightgown slipped down over one shoulder, baring the top of her breast to his view. The hem of the garment was hiked up high across her thighs, drawing his immediate and total attention.

Cat could only imagine how she must look to him with her legs spread out against the cool, white linen sheets and her half-exposed chest heaving furiously. If his gaze was anything to go by, she undoubtedly made a pretty interesting picture. So fascinating in fact, that he continued to undress the rest of her with his eyes, visually removing what scant clothing she had left.

Now, Cat told herself, was the time to make her move, to take advantage of his preoccupation and bolt straight out the door and back down to the safe, reassuring sanctity of her bedroom. But she didn't do so much as twitch a muscle. Not out of helplessness, or hopelessness, or sheer, abject, maidenly terror. *Curiosity* was what kept her riveted to the spot.

Foolish, wanton, female curiosity.

She wanted to stick around for a while to see what happened.

His gaze darkened, sliding roughly over her naked skin, bold as a physical touch. Her flesh shivered, responding as if he had stroked her there, where the silk of her gown met the crest of her legs. She exhaled slowly, loving the feel of it, wondering how no more than a look from him could make her so weak.

"What are you going to do?" she whispered.

"Everything," he promised, breathing more sensual meaning into the single word than Cat could ever be prepared for.

Starlight poured in through the picture window, highlighting the dark strands of his hair with soft, silver fire. Ocean waves lapped against the shore outside, making slow, ancient music as they played in and out between the shifting hills of sand. The air was wet and heavy, thick with early-morning mist.

His hand was warm against her breast when he

touched her there. He took the silk strap of her nightie in his clasp, drawing it down until the soft, swollen mound overflowed against his fingers. His breathing raced as he studied what he'd exposed.

His reaction reminded Cat just who was in control.

No one.

He took the second shoulder strap between his teeth and worked the remaining material down, seductively baring her other breast. Cat was aware of several sensations at once—the length of his hair, tickling against her, the sensual pressure of the fabric as it pulled, finally giving way. The unexpected pleasure as he explored each peak with the surface of his tongue, kissing first one, then the other in turn.

Muscles clutched deep inside her. Diego's touch was so raw and tender, it was all Cat could do to keep from crying out. If he had been rough or impatient, she might have had some hope of resisting.

But he wasn't rough. He took his time as he tasted her, wetting her breasts with his lazy, languid kisses, taking her taut nipples into his mouth and suckling for what seemed like an eternity.

In heaven.

Twining her fingers wildly through his hair, Cat strained toward him, instinctively pressing him closer, holding on for dear life. She was trembling, she realized, parting like the frail petals of a flower, unfolding to the light. Diego was shaking as well, as if the power of what was happening between them was even stronger than he had expected.

But still he didn't stop. His mouth continued teasing, stroking, lathing at the pleasure-swollen pink aureoles until she was ready to weep from the searing, sweet longing. A gentle wind blew over the dampness of her skin, pebbling the darkened centers to tight peaks.

Groaning at the sight of her, Diego redoubled his efforts, flicking his tongue across the hardened tips until they burned with the sharp, stinging pleasure of it, making her wet everywhere. Wet and warm with the most intense wanting she'd ever felt.

A soft whimper escaped her.

"*Cara*," he breathed, pulling back to look at her. "You are beautiful."

The ache in Cat's throat was so tight, she could barely swallow. *He* was beautiful. So handsome, it almost hurt to look at him.

And the way he was looking at her! If ever a man could make love with his eyes, this one could. He drank her in deeply with his turbulent gaze, enveloping her with wave after wave of unspeakable desire. If looks could seduce, Cat figured she'd already been captivated. And if he could enrapture her so thoroughly with a single glance, what would happen when he—?

All thoughts flew suddenly out of her head as Diego closed his hands on her shoulders, coaxing her gently upward and into his arms. Cat's heart rocketed when she realized he was going to kiss her.

Cat knew she should turn him away, because anything less would signal her complete and unconditional surrender. At the very minimum, she should stop herself from responding. But she couldn't. Instead of turning her face the other way, she sank into his arms and lifted her mouth up to meet him.

The moment their lips touched, Cat finally understood what real ravishing was. It wasn't about fear or force. It was about this. A mind-melting, completely mutual kiss. A physical connection so complete that her emotions were laid as bare as her body.

His hands splayed across her face, stroking her cheeks softly, caressing her skin with the tips of his fingers as sensitively as his mouth had ministered to her breasts. Cat felt her heart squeeze tight. It wasn't only his eyes that Diego knew how to make love with.

She was kissing him back, helpless to stop herself, lost in the solid male warmth of him. Losing herself to a fantasy.

Captain Diego Swift. *He* was the fantasy, the most daring, reckless, dangerous man she had ever met, but also the most real. He might be something of a scoundrel on the surface, but underneath, his honor was totally intact. In fact, he had far more of that than any modern man she'd ever met.

With a rogue like Diego, the civilized veneer was stripped away, leaving only the pure, male essence of the man. He was angry or proud, curious or passionate, all with an honest, unvarnished intensity. In fact, there was so *much* male essence where Diego was involved, Cat wasn't sure how to handle him. His survival instincts were strong, *he* was strong, but at the same time far too innocent for her world. He didn't even belong in her world.

Or in her life, for that matter.

How long would it take him to figure that out? What was to stop him from roving again as soon as he got good and ready?

She was the one who had to stop herself now, before their lovemaking went too far. The consequences were simply too great to risk for a single night of gratification. No matter how much she might want to take that risk with him.

He deepened the kiss, overwhelming her with the incredible intensity of it. Cat pulled back with an effort, trying to catch her breath.

"I'm sorry," she whispered, dropping her head against his chest. "We can't do this. *I* can't do this."

SIX

Instead of reacting to her words in anger, as Cat had expected, Diego cradled her even closer. One large hand was caressing her hair while the other closed tightly around her waist, holding on as though he would never let go. Hands that were shaking slightly, Cat realized. It had been as difficult for him to stop the kiss as it had been for her.

Maybe even more difficult, if his ragged breathing and hold on her were anything to go by. But he had stopped himself. He was holding back for her sake, a gesture that posed a greater threat to her emotions than all the ravishing in the world.

"I have frightened you, Catalina," he finally said when his breathing had begun to steady a bit, "have I not?"

Cat winced at the edge of pain she heard in his tone. Was it physical or mental, or maybe a little bit of both? Either way, she had caused it. How could she hope to explain that it wasn't his lovemaking that had frightened her, but rather her own response to it?

"I am scared," she admitted. "But it's not what you think. I—I've only been with a man once before, when I was sixteen."

"So young, *cara*. Was it a poor experience? Did the cad fail to please you?"

She made no move to look up at him. It was hard enough to relate what had happened without staring into those all-seeing eyes. Even now, when she was old enough to realize she'd done nothing worse than give in to some serious adolescent hormones, the shame of that night still lingered.

"He was a senior I'd been dating from the local high school," she explained. "The nuns forbade me to see him, but we snuck away one night—they caught us. It was *awful*. I felt like I'd finally lived up to every low expectation the sisters had for me. I guess they thought so, too, since they suspended me from school for a week."

She'd never had the nerve to get physical since. Nor the inclination, until now. Would Diego understand all that?

"Such evil luck, Catalina, that you should have been discovered. I am truly sorry for it. But you are still an innocent. Losing your virginity to a mere boy is likely worse than having no physical experience at all."

Rearranging her nightie back over her shoulders, she glanced shyly up at him. "You do understand."

"Did you think me incapable of compassion, lass?" he questioned, still stroking the back of her head. "My heart does beat every now and then, I swear." As if to prove his point, he caught her hand in his and held it against his warm chest wall, a little to the left of center.

The firm, steady thudding Cat felt there made her own heart go a little weak.

"Alive and well," she whispered.

"Aye, Catalina. Even though you have come close to killing me, sweet. Do your modern doctors know whether or not it is possible for a man to expire from need of a woman?"

"I—believe it's unlikely."

He caught her hand again and kissed it. "Then I am safe here awhile longer."

Cat felt the warmth of him stealing into her fingers as he splayed them playfully across his face, touching each sensitive tip to his lips in turn. "Physical love," he said, "can be most pleasant with a man who knows what he's doing, *cara*. When you are ready, I want to be that man for you."

Pleasant? Cat thought. That was exactly what worried her. With a man like Diego, lovemaking would be nothing short of explosive. She knew who would pay the price for it in the end. Heaven help her, she *knew*.

What if she did go through with it? Her entire life had been the consequence of just such a mistake. *She* was living proof of her own parents' misjudgment.

Free love? In Cat's experience, it wasn't free. It had cost her plenty. How could she take the chance of falling for a man committed only to adventure?

She *couldn't*, that was the only possible answer. The only love she planned on making with any man was the legal, till-death-do-us-part, sign-on-the-dotted-line kind of love. The kind that Diego was incapable of giving her.

Gently, with more regret than she'd thought herself capable of feeling, she pulled her hand away. "I'm sorry," she said softly. "Please understand, but I'll never be ready for what you're describing. And you will never be that man."

"Another shot of rum, mate," Diego instructed the bartender, staring at the brownish-amber liquid as it was slowly decanted from the crystal bottle into the small glass before him. Dark rum it was, the island-brewed kind made to cure a man's woes with a single swallow. Kill them dead as it were.

In his case, however, he'd had several long swallows already, and it still hadn't eased what was ailing him. Catalina Steadwell. The woman was a vexation that hundred-proof whiskey was too weak to handle.

He raised the shot glass to his lips, tossing back another searing swig of the stuff, hoping to hell and back that it might bring him some kind of relief.

It didn't.

The alcohol burned a fiery path from his throat to his belly, but nothing, he knew, had the power to slake the slow burn that she had kindled inside him. Nothing, except a long night alone with Cat.

A night she had promised him would never come to pass.

Diego swore viciously at the memory, making the man on the bar stool beside him jump. So much for the seduction he'd planned. Somehow, Catalina had managed to resist his most valiant efforts at making himself irresistible.

Nay, it was even worse than that. He had given in to that resistance he felt in her, letting his sails slacken when he should have been heading straight into the wind. For the first time in his life, he had turned the wheel over to a female. And she was slowly steering him straight for the lunatic asylum.

Marriage was what she'd spoken of in the midst of their lovemaking. Wedded bliss was what Ms. Steadwell wanted *before* she was bedded. The only sort of bliss a pirate such as he could not provide her.

Diego Swift, married? Had the woman gone completely mad? Else why would she even suggest such a thing?

Of course, it clearly hadn't been him she'd had in mind while suggesting it. Pirates plainly were not known for making fine husbands, and he was certainly no exception to that age-old rule. He would not even have a clear idea how to go about keeping only one woman happy.

Indeed, he had learned the most about male-female relationships from growing up in the bordello. He had seen the many men his mother had lain with. He had seen those men leave, one by one. And while it had pained him to watch the endless procession, he had simply assumed that it was a normal way of life. It was not until he had chased his own father halfway round the world for hurting his mother that he realized not all men were such mongrels.

Still, he himself was born from that man, was he not? Did that not make him half a mongrel himself, incapable of caring deeply for a woman? Aye, that was why he had turned to piracy in the first place. Not only to avenge his father's sins, *but because he had believed himself to be good for nothing better.*

And he was still good for nothing.

Swashbucklers did not settle down and live happily ever after. They did not deserve to.

Did they?

Nay, he decided, slamming the shot glass down on the ale-house counter with a force that made the bloke beside him slink silently away. Perhaps that was the sort of Milquetoast mate that Catalina wanted to wed. The kind that she could easily order about, one who would relinquish all control to the whims of a strong-minded female, just so he might partake of her considerable charms.

What the devil did a man such as that have, that he, celebrate historical icon of the high seas, did not?

An occupation, for one thing, he decided regretfully. The current *job market* for pirates was pretty much dried up and showed no signs of improving in the near future. Of what use was a man who no longer had a purpose in life?

Being captain of a tourist or fishing boat was the only career he might qualify for, after some small amount of training, but neither one was much to his taste. What kind of husband would he make for Catalina if he could not even find himself gainful employment? No man of honor would allow his wife to wear the pants in his family. And no matter how provocative his sweet looked in pants, his own doubtful illusion of honor was all he had left.

A husband? Oh hell, he was not even trifling with the thought of marrying her, was he? Nay, it was an idea he had not the luxury to consider in light of his current situation. At least, he was not at liberty to wed Cat legally.

He did not even exist legally.

He had no *birth certificate*. No *Social Security number*. These were items which Cat had explained were required of a man to live in society today. Important articles which he had little hope of obtaining.

The *Social Security office* was unlikely to hand over a number to him at the point of a sword. How else was he expected to secure one if not by straightforward seizing? A sorry piece of work it was when a buccaneer could not even capture what he needed.

Nay, he was not even a swashbuckler any longer. He was an *illegal alien*. A creature, in fact, which the dictionary told him was not only from a foreign land, but possibly from another planet. A barbarian who did not belong.

In the midst of mulling over these pressing problems, he had barely taken notice of the two ladies sidling up to the bar on either side of him. He could hardly fail to make note of them now as one slid onto the bar stool which Mr. Milquetoast had deserted and the other leaned so close to his left shoulder that a puff of air could not be blown between them.

"Buy us a drink, sailor?" she suggested, smiling provocatively.

Diego glanced from one to the other, deciding dispassionately that they were far from bad-looking *babes*. Attractively garbed these *chicks* were as well, with clothes that could not fail to catch a man's eye. Short skirts, low-slung tops, and another amazing modern invention, *high heels*.

Neither did he miss the come-hither looks they were sending his way. Ladies of the evening, that's what these wenches were. Women he wanted no part of.

"Sorry, babe," he said, hoping they would leave him alone, "but this sailor has no coins nor credit cards."

The girl on his right giggled. "Then maybe we should buy *you* a drink."

Diego's eyebrows went up. What were these persistent lasses after if not his dollars? "Some other time," he said firmly.

Shrugging their shoulders in disappointment, they stood to leave. "Some time *soon*," the one on his right whispered. "Nice buns."

Diego stared after them in confusion as they disappeared out the door, presumably to round up a bit of better-paying business.

He signaled to the barkeep. "Listen, mate," he said, as the man leaned over. "What is the significance of *buns*?"

"Buns?" the man repeated.

"Aye!" Diego exclaimed. "*Buns*. That babe said I had nice ones."

"Sport," the bartender said, "are you from another planet or something?"

"Aye," Diego responded ruefully, "I have been told as much."

"Man, you must be! Don't you know when a couple of lookers are trying to pick you up?"

"*Pick me up?*"

"Wanted you bad, sport. Two of them at once, you lucky jerk."

Diego narrowed his eyes in disbelief. "Am I to understand that those lasses were offering their services for free?"

"You got it, bub. Coupla cool chicks out cruising. Man, you gotta *love* wild women like that!"

"I do?"

"Well, no, you don't *have* to. Aw hell, buddy, I give up. You're hopeless."

Aye, Diego agreed, watching the bartender walk away, shaking his head slowly. He was a *dude* without hope. He did not even care to sample the charms of those two lovely women, no matter if the cost was nothing.

It was a sorry state he was in, indeed, when fine

ladies such as that held no sway over him. Free ladies, his for the taking, and he still had no inclination. Sexually promiscuous, that's what those modern
females were. This century, it seemed, was a sailor's
dream come true.

But what was the good of a hundred loose
wenches when the single one you wanted fancied
wedlock? Catalina Steadwell. Aye, it was just his luck
to land smack-dab in a century full of unrestrained
cyprians and end up falling for an old-fashioned girl.

Tossing a tip to the bartender, he stood to take his
leave, strolling back out onto the sidewalk toward the
house. It was late in the afternoon already, and Catalina's all-important meeting with the preservation
board was scheduled to start at three o'clock. In spite
of her suggestion that he might not be at ease taking
tea with a group of hard-to-please, beautification-
minded biddies, Diego was determined to be there.

Aye, if he could not have Catalina, at least he
could help her. Winning the board's approval meant
so much to her, it had grown to be nearly as important to him. With further funding, she could afford
to stay in the house as long as she pleased, and con-
tinue restoring to her heart's content.

A sudden question rose, unbidden, in his mind.
Would he be equally pleased to remain there with
her? And for how long would he wish to stay?

Forever?

It was an answer he was not yet prepared to give.
Too many complications remained unresolved between them, as did his own position in this new

twentieth-century society. Cars whizzed past him on the busy city street at a pace that still made him marvel. So much was different in this day of full-speed everything. A man was expected to adapt as quickly, or be left by the wayside.

Diego did not doubt he was capable of adapting, but before settling on what his own future should be, he wanted to assist Catalina in resolving hers. Although she did not seem to realize it, he could be of some use to her in winning the board members to their side.

The meeting was already in progress by the time he arrived back at the house. He stopped momentarily outside an open window to assess how things were going inside. Not too well, from what he could make out.

Catalina had been entirely correct in her appraisal of the board members. Never had Diego seen a more withered bunch of haughty, humorless women in his life. Many were well advanced in age, but it wasn't their beauty that had shriveled with the years, it was their spirit.

There seemed to be no zest for life remaining in the lot of them. They barely reacted to Catalina's obvious enthusiasm as she poured steaming cups of tea for them into fragile china cups and carefully recited the architectural and historical merits of the building. Aye, his sweet was doing a fine job of putting her facts and figures before them, but not one of the members seemed moved by her presentation. Several were glancing down at their watches with greater interest than they had spent in studying the room they were in.

Diego decided he had to do something quickly, or Catalina's cause would be sunk for sure. He strolled up the front steps and swaggered boldly into the midst of them.

"Ladies," he said, dropping the surprised group a fine flourish of a bow. "It is a pleasure, indeed, to make your acquaintance. I have been looking forward to meeting all of you for some time now."

Catalina shot him a warning look, but seemed grateful for his appearance all the same.

"Ms. Steadwell," he said, "would you mind making these charming ladies known to me? *My* name," he added softly, speaking to Catalina in a low whisper, "can be of little importance compared to theirs. There is surely no reason to reveal it."

Catalina managed to make the introductions without revealing his identity, although she was clearly having an awkward time of it. Diego was simply pleased that she trusted him enough to comply with his request.

She personally presented each board member to him, one at a time, as he heartily shook their coolly outstretched hands. Every eyebrow in the room was raised by the time they neared the end of the group. Clearly his sudden appearance had piqued their curiosity, if nothing more. At least they wanted to know exactly who he was and what business, if any, he had there.

The chairwoman herself, the formidable Mrs.

Grimlet, was the last person Catalina introduced to him. The sharp-eyed old woman reluctantly held out her long, grasping fingers.

"And who might you be?" she demanded, glancing speculatively from Diego to Catalina and back again. "The hired help?"

"Exactly, ma'am," he agreed politely. "No more than a humble handyman who has been assisting Ms. Steadwell restore this fine old house in exchange for room and board." But instead of gripping her hand for a friendly shake, he brought the crinkled fingertips to his lips and kissed them.

Catalina wondered if Mrs. Grimlet was going to faint. From the flush that had spread across her pale, formerly lifeless face and the way her eyelashes were fluttering, it was clear that Diego's smooth move had caught her off guard. But it was nearly impossible to tell from her shuttered expression whether she approved of the gesture or not. Or of the man who had made it.

"Oh?" she finally managed in response. "You live here, then, sir?"

"Aye," Diego acknowledged calmly, commandeering the teapot from Catalina and attentively topping off Mrs. Grimlet's cup. "But, please," he added, flashing her a heart-stopping smile, "call me *señor*."

Mrs. Grimlet's delicate porcelain teacup rattled gently against its saucer. "Very well, then," she agreed, flustered in spite of herself. "Señor. I *thought* I detected a Spanish accent in your voice."

"Very clever of you," Diego said, relinquishing

the teapot and settling himself audaciously on the arm of Mrs. Grimlet's chair. "You are quite correct, of course. It is my first language. And I knew instantly that you were a woman of superior taste and refinement. Indeed, who else would be able to see the great beauty hidden in such a weathered old house as this?"

The older woman glanced doubtfully around the room. Diego's charm had started to thaw her out for a second there, but apparently, she remained unconvinced as to the merits of the house. "Perhaps there *was* something special in the building," she admitted, "long ago. But I'm afraid much of it has been lost through the years. As well as much being added that does not belong. The widow's walk along the roof, for instance. A Victorian-era vanity that is most certainly not original."

"But that's part of the charm," Cat protested.

"Maybe," Mrs. Grimlet said sternly, "but it is shockingly inaccurate. And I see no other features in the structure that would warrant our involvement at this time."

Several of the other members began to nod in agreement. Some of them stood to leave. They hadn't even seen the whole place yet! Cat thought in sickening frustration, and they were already prepared to walk out the door, taking her dreams along with them.

"But I cannot allow you to go," Diego cut in, his voice smooth and low, lethally polite.

Cat swallowed hard as all eyes turned toward

him. Oh dear. What was he going to do, now? Hold
the reluctant board members there against their will
until they came around to his way of thinking? A
disconcerting vision of Mrs. Grimlet, bound and
gagged and stashed secretly in the attic, popped suddenly into her mind.

"Until you hear the earliest history of the house,"
he added calmly, "and the dastardly details of the
swashbuckler who built it."

Cat wasn't sure whether to breathe a sigh of relief
or hold her breath for what was to come.

"A swashbuckler?" one of the women breathed,
horrified. "Never say a *pirate* lived here?"

"Not a mere pirate," Diego told her, warming to
his tale, "the wickedest scoundrel of a sailor that ever
traveled Florida's Treasure Coast. Captain Diego
Swift." He swept his cool, searching blue eyes
around the room. "But, surely you ladies have heard
of him?"

From that point on, Cat realized, Diego had
them in his pocket. The story he related of the infamous Captain Swift was so wildly shocking and juicy
that not even Mrs. Grimlet could resist being se-
duced by it. Of course, she suspected not even half of
it was true, but in the end, it was more than enough
to establish a deep and abiding fascination for the
house in the board members' minds.

The tour Diego gave them of the attic was certainly the clincher. It was the very spot, he assured
them, where the roguish, ruthless Diego Swift had
held more than a dozen women captive as his per-

sonal love slaves. Mrs. Roselyn had passed out at the idea of it and had to be carried down to the first floor by Diego himself.

If she only knew! Cat mused. The true Diego wasn't nearly as fearsome or horrifying as he made himself out to be, but he was there with them right now. Alive and well and plying his charm to the hilt.

"Of course, this changes everything," Mrs. Grimlet assured them. "It would be unthinkable to let a structure of so much social significance fall into ruin." She smiled warmly at Catalina. "You can certainly count on our financial support, my dear, but you should have *told* me that the house came with such an unusual provenance."

"Believe me," Catalina said, "I had no idea who Diego Swift was when I bought the place. But I'm starting to get a pretty good idea."

SEVEN

As soon as the door shut behind Mrs. Grimlet and the other members of the beautification board, Cat threw her arms around Diego's neck and hugged him hard. "I could kiss you!" she told him, elated.

"Be my guest, lass," he invited warmly.

Recalled to her senses by the intimate words, she checked her impulse and drew back. "Sorry," she murmured, "it was just a figure of speech."

"Was it, sweet?"

"Yes. I'm so grateful for what you just did. Diego, you saved my house! I mean your house. I—Oh, you know what I mean!"

"Indeed. You are, in fact, pleased with me."

"I'm thrilled!" she told him. "How can I ever thank you?"

He raked a hand slowly across the five-o'clock shadow on his chin. "I'm sure we might think of something. But then again, I did not do it for your thanks, Catalina. I simply wished to help."

She did kiss him then, gently, on one stubble-rough cheek. "Thank you," she said, "you were wonderful."

"I was," he agreed.

"I thought Mrs. Roselyn's eyes were going to pop out of her head. And Mrs. Grimlet—she actually winked at you! If you ever want to start an affair with a rich older woman, I think she's ready. But then, she might find out who you really are. The dreaded *Diablo.*"

"Aye," he agreed, "I suppose I dare not risk discovery of my true, evil identity."

"I see what you mean," Cat said. "In fact, now that we've gone public with Captain Swift's story, it might not be such a good idea for you to be running around town telling everyone your name."

"Nay," he said. "In fact, they would not believe me even though I speak the truth."

"A new name is what you need," Cat decided, thinking out loud. "But why stop there? If we do this thing right, we might be able to get you a whole new identity. A birth certificate. A Social Security card. The works."

Diego looked down at her, grinning in undisguised approval. "Now, Catalina, you are plotting like a true pirate. But exactly how are we to acquire these contraband documents?"

"Simple," she told him. "We start at the library."

———◆———

They were seated side by side in the back corner of the microfilm room, poring over the second tape of newspaper obituaries from 1959 when Diego finally demanded a full explanation.

Growing impatient with the tedium of the task Catalina had set for them, he kicked back in his industrial-strength library chair and folded his arms behind his head, waiting for her to find the needle in the haystack.

"Lass," he said, lowering his voice to a smooth whisper that would not be overheard, "how do you know that this will work?"

"I'm a historian, remember?" she reminded him gently, without lifting her eyes from the rapidly scrolling screen. "I do research for a living. If there's one thing I know about, it's dead people and the documents they leave behind."

"Indeed," Diego agreed. "It took you little time to discover the facts pertaining to my own unfortunate—demise. But I still fail to see how you can produce a birth certificate for me where none has existed before."

"All we have to do," Catalina explained, "is find the right obituary on this microfilm. We need a boy who was born thirty-nine years ago, but died a few years later, preferably out of state. That boy's birth certificate should still be on file here in Florida, since the different states don't normally share their old birth and death information with one another. We write to the County Clerk's Office in Jacksonville, send in our nine-dollar-document-replacement fee for an official copy of that certificate, and bingo, two weeks later, you're legally recognized as someone else."

She stopped scrolling through the records momentarily, leaning forward to read a particular blurry green paragraph more easily. "Right year," she told him, "wrong name. You don't look much like a Eustacia to me."

"Eustacia?" Diego repeated doubtfully. "I am relieved, Catalina, that you do not wish to saddle me with such an unlikely name. In fact it seems something of a shame that I must give up my own. Is there no other way?"

"None that I can think of," she told him honestly. "It's really kind of an exciting opportunity for you, though, Diego. Not many people have a chance to start over again, with a clean slate."

Aye, she was right about that, Diego decided. A new start in life was an opportunity to make amends for a past he had never been especially proud of. But would it really be possible for a pirate such as he to reform his wandering, plundering ways? Were they not second nature to him, character flaws that had been passed down to him by the man who had sired him? Had he not inherited those traits from his so-called father? Or was it realistic to hope that he might rise above them, and live a respectable life in spite of his parental history?

"I suppose I did not look at it in that way before,

Catalina," he admitted. "But now that you bring it up, it might not be such a bad thing to leave Diego Swift behind and attempt to live a more honorable life as a new man. More's the pity I cannot choose new parents for myself as well."

"New parents?" she asked, turning to look at him.

It was the tone of Diego's voice that made Cat wonder what he was thinking. Something still seemed to be bothering him, holding him back from searching for a new name with the kind of enthusiasm she'd expected. But it wasn't only the name he was looking to change, she realized. It was his identity. His life.

"Aye," he agreed. "You remember what I told you about my father, Catalina, do you not?"

"Of course," she assured him. "But what does he have to do with our search?"

"I would prefer the bloody bastard had *nothing* to do with it," he said, "but I am not sure that I can ever be rid of the legacy he has left me. Catalina, do you believe it is inevitable for a son to inherit the father's sins?"

Cat hesitated. Was that what was troubling him? Was he worried that his destiny had been predetermined by the undesirable qualities of the man who had fathered him? "I believe," she said slowly, "that a person can choose any course they want in life. Diego, you told me once you became a pirate to punish your father for what he had done to your mother.

Are you sure it wasn't to fulfill the low expectations you had for yourself?"

"He was a bad man," Diego said quietly. "Does it not follow that I must turn out a scoundrel as well?"

"No," Cat insisted. "It does not."

"How do you know this?" he demanded, his expression intent, full of a pain he was rarely vulnerable enough to reveal.

"Because that's exactly what the Sisters of Mercy always thought about me," she said softly. "They were certain I would turn out like my mother. Rebellious. Impulsive. A little wild and irresponsible. They punished me for showing any signs of those traits, and after a while I learned to suppress them completely. But Diego, they were wrong. I'm nothing like her. In fact, I think it would probably do me some good to be a little *more* impulsive. You've taught me that."

"I, Catalina? How?"

"By showing me that being cautious and reserved sometimes has its downside. I was so worried about what the women on the beautification board would think that I stifled myself completely. I was boring them to tears before you came along and livened things up."

He nodded slowly, apparently finding some useful shred of wisdom in what she'd said. He caught her hand and squeezed it hard. "Perhaps," he told her, "there is hope for both of us yet. Keep searching, sweet. Surely we can do better than Eustacia."

Catalina grinned, resuming the hunt for a more

appropriate name. Several pages later she found another candidate. "Here's one," she said, smiling. "Eleazar Jones. It's perfect!"

"Eleazar!" Diego exclaimed, groaning. "Perfect, Catalina? Do you think so, indeed? Does this look like the face of a man named Eleazar?"

He turned his haughty, handsome profile toward her, and Cat burst out laughing.

"Don't worry," she assured him. "I was just teasing. Listen, here's the real name, and I think it truly is perfect. Douglas Smith. You won't even have to change your initials."

"Douglas," he repeated, trying the sound of it on for size. "Aye, it is not a bad one as far as names go. Douglas Smith I shall be, then. How long do you imagine it will take to get the birth certificate?"

"Two to three weeks according to the Jacksonville office," she informed him, copying down Douglas's vital information. "That should give us both some time to adjust before the change is official. After that, we'll go for the Social Security number. Meanwhile, I think we should do something to celebrate. What do you say, Mr. Smith?"

Diego grinned. "Precisely what I was thinking, Ms. Steadwell. And I believe I know exactly what that something should be."

Cat did a double take when she first set eyes on the boat that Diego had rented for the day. He'd invited her out for an "easy voyage" for their celebration, the last official voyage that Diego Swift the pirate would ever make. Cat had naively imagined this would have something to do with a small, quiet sort of sailboat. Maybe a two-seater catamaran that the wind would blow lightly around the harbor and down around the picturesque southern tip of Bird Island.

She'd been wrong.

She should've known that a reckless spirit like Diego wouldn't settle for anything as tame as a sailboat once the treasure chest of twentieth-century technology had been pried open for him. No self-respecting buccaneer would be caught dead in an outdated wooden dinghy when there was a brave new world of fiberglass at his fingertips. Metallic-blue fiberglass to be precise, with a flaming black racing stripe running from bow to stern.

A thirty-foot powerboat, that's what Captain Swift had commandeered for the day cruise. A long, sleek, fuel-injected monster of a racing vessel. This pirate, apparently, preferred flying to coasting. He was an old-fashioned swashbuckler with a very modern need for speed.

Clutching her straw beach basket in one hand and the wide, wooden dock railing with the other, Cat balanced her sandal-clad feet precariously on the edge of the ramp as he helped her into the bobbing boat. Seconds later, they were pushing away, idling down the narrow canal that led from Crazy Al's You-Buy-It-We-Sell-It Boatyard to the scenic Intracoastal Waterway.

Diego flashed her a grin, apparently having no problem in the driving department, although it was hard to say for certain with his eyes hidden behind a pair of mirrored sunglasses. That, along with the pineapple-motif swim trunks, the neon-yellow cord trailing from his ponytail, and the ever-present gold earring, gave him a lazy, laid-back, Caribbean kind of look. Half rugged sea captain, half Big Kahuna.

Cat wondered if this day of unbridled celebration was such a good idea after all. The morning was bright, the sky was blue. The man beside her was unbearably sexy.

Anything could happen.

"I hope you didn't spend your entire paycheck on this," she said, indicating the flashy blue craft they were cruising in. "It must've cost a fortune just to rent it."

He leaned back confidently in his seat, steering the boat with only one hand as he shrugged a careless answer to her question. "Nay, Catalina. Not a single silver peso."

She shot him a sudden, surprised glance. "You mean it was—free?"

He smiled again, flicked his long black ponytail over his shoulder and threw his head back to take in the cloudless August sky. "As the white seagulls flying overhead."

"Diego, you didn't—" It occurred to her briefly that he'd simply seized the vessel back at Crazy Al's. Driven it away, in fact, without Al's or anyone else's permission. She cast a worried glance in the rearview mirror, wondering if the coast guard would be bearing down on them at any moment.

"Settle down, sweet," he suggested. "I did not pilfer it, if that's what has your busy brain in such a whirl. Crazy Al himself provided me my first *private lesson* and thereafter handed me the key."

"But—oh dear. Do you suppose—Does he think you bought it?"

"Nay, I as much as told him the amount he asked was far too high for a craft that had been previously sailed."

"Previously sailed? Oh. So, it's a used boat? Well, that makes it a *little* better."

Diego nodded, idly experimenting with the give-and-take of the throttle as though he could hardly wait to power up his new toy. "Crazy Al promised to plunge the price after my *test drive*."

"I'll bet," Cat commented, rolling her eyes. "Does he have any idea we're going to be gone the entire day?"

"Aye. He said I should *bring this baby back to him by tomorrow*."

"I see . . ." Cat still didn't feel entirely right about borrowing the boat for a whole day when she knew very well Diego couldn't afford it. Although it was a major relief to know he hadn't simply pirated the thing away. But when Crazy Al discovered that the captain's credit rating was nonexistent, he really was going to go crazy.

"Some fine *chick magnet* this is, eh Catalina?" Diego asked her, patting the streamlined dashboard as though it were a temperamental thoroughbred that would respond only to his confident brand of coaxing.

"Excuse me?"

"A boat with *room for about a dozen broads in tight bikinis.*"

"*Broads?*" Cat repeated, beginning to get a good idea of the sleazy salesman's questionable technique. "Is *that* what Crazy Al said?"

Diego nodded. "With a vessel that can hold so many, I knew you and I would not be crowded."

Cat settled back into her plush leather seat, feeling no further qualms for creepy Al. For all she knew, Diego *was* thinking about purchasing the boat. On the hundred-year payment plan.

Meanwhile, this bikini-clad broad was going to sit back and enjoy the ride. The sun felt warm and wonderful against her shoulders, the cover-up T-shirt she wore, too hot. She peeled it off, dipping into her basket for a bottle of sunscreen.

The sound of Diego's voice stopped her short. It was low and rusty, rough with intimacy.

"That is a beautiful brassiere you are wearing, lass."

She glanced toward him. The look on his face made her swallow with sudden awareness. His eyes had gone breathtakingly blue, the dark lashes shuttered, scanning her body with searing approval.

"Bra—oh. No, Diego, this is my bathing-suit top."

He seemed puzzled.

"A *bathing suit*," he repeated. "How can this be, *cara*? One is nearly identical to the other."

"Well, I imagine it must *look* that way," she admitted, glancing down at her top and trying to imagine how it must appear from his perspective. If anything, the suit was *skimpier* than any undergarment she owned. There was no lace, no bows, no thin fabric padding to cover the telltale feminine bumps and bulges of her body. There was only a small stretch of space-age fabric, so thin, it was hard to tell where the suit left off and her own skin began. She was practically *exposed*, for heaven's sake! At least, that's how it felt with him studying her that way.

"Technically," she said, struggling for words, "well, you see—it's a little hard to explain. A bra is usually lacy and worn *under* something, unless of course, you're a rock star or fashion model, or just in a basically daring mood. But a bathing suit top—spandex in this case—is considered okay for public view."

His eyes had practically burned a hole in her suit straight through to her tingling flesh before his gaze lifted and locked with hers. "It is okay by me, Catalina."

A soft flush spread across her face and shoulders at his words. "Thank you."

"But there are still many words I do not understand the meaning of."

"Oh?"

"Aye," he admitted. "Words such as *buns*, for instance."

"Buns?" She hesitated. "Hmmm . . . Well, in a case like that, I'd say context is everything."

"Indeed?"

"Right. A lot depends on how it was used in the sentence? You know—'A dozen baked buns, please.' 'Those buns are hot.' 'What delicious buns.' "

He stroked his chin slowly. "Nay," he said, "it was none of those. It was simply, 'Nice buns.' "

The light of comprehension began to dawn in Cat's mind. "Oh. Nice buns, huh? Who said that?"

"A wench at the corner alehouse."

"Referring to *your* buns, no doubt," Cat said dryly, experiencing a pang of territorial jealousy so sharp, it nearly took her breath away.

What did she care if some brazen hussy down at the local bar tried to fling herself at Diego, anyway? He was a free agent. Community property. She had no right to stop some other woman from admiring the view. She simply had the overwhelming urge to punch the cheap tart's lights out.

"In that case," she continued, striving for calm, "she was referring to your—your . . ."

"My—"

"Well, not your fore, but your . . . aft."

There was a long pause while he seemed to absorb this interesting bit of information. "Now it is becoming clear to me," he told her finally. "The barkeep said *they wanted me bad*."

"*They?*" Cat repeated. "You mean there was more than one?"

"It makes little difference, Catalina," he stated flatly. "They did not interest me."

"Oh?" she said, congratulating herself on not falling onto the deck of the boat and shouting a sincere, grateful prayer on the spot.

"Nay, lass. Do you not know that by now?"

"I—wasn't sure."

Diego was only beginning to get a clear idea, himself, that Catalina was the one and only woman he wanted.

Lifelong monogamy was a thought nearly as foreign to him as this new life he was just beginning to adjust to. Funny, but it was her *bathing-suit* top that had made him truly start to consider the idea.

If ever there was a provocative garment designed to catch a man's roving eye, it was that one. There was hardly more than an inch or two of silky, soft material to the entire getup. A mantrap, that's what it was. A stretchy, slinky cradle of a miraculous fiber called *spandex*. Surely the fabric had to be worth more than its weight in precious gems. Was that why they only made use of it in such minuscule amounts?

Catalina had said it was a perfectly acceptable item of clothing to wear. Acceptable? It was dangerous. It seemed there was no end to the cruelly sensuous inventions of this new century.

And therein lay the rub.

The most miraculous achievement of all was the fact that he had seen the lovely Catalina in such a garment and actually managed to keep his pirate paws off her. For the time being, anyway. That was true progress of sorts, was it not? Perhaps he was already behaving more like the decent fellow, Douglas Smith, than the swashbuckler, Diego.

Still, he preferred not to press his luck. A distraction was what he needed to keep his mind off such fascinating details. Aye, there was nothing like the thought of an excellent lunch to stave off the threat of involuntary lechery.

Guiding the boat into a quiet cove, he pulled the *throttle* back to the stop position and cut the engine.

Catalina stirred in her seat. "What are we doing?"

"All this fresh air has made me hungry, sweet," he explained, retrieving a *cooler* from the spot beneath the bow where he'd stowed it. "I am stopping to prepare you an 'alfresco' lunch."

"A pirate with a flair for picnics?" she teased, abandoning her seat and approaching the ice chest with curiosity. "Great. I'm starving. What are we having?"

"Some wine to begin with?" he suggested, pulling a dark green bottle from the cool depths of the icebox and expertly uncorking it. "A *Sercial* Madeira, fortified with brandy, *cara*. Light as rainwater, golden as the glow in your eyes. I'm told this vintage was a very good year. One of many that I seem to have missed."

Laughing, she took the full glass he offered and

raised it in the air for a toast. "To all the years still *ahead* then," she suggested.

"Aye," he agreed, ringing his goblet against hers, "to those."

"But I'm still hungry," she told him, taking another step forward, trying to peer into the cooler. "What else have you got hiding in there?"

"Bread and cheese," he said, taking out a long, crusty French loaf and a small white wheel of Brie. "Fruit as well, lass. Oranges as sweet as I've ever seen. Strawberries that must've been grown for the gods, so red and ripe they are. Mangoes, peaches. I was tempted to take along the entire *grocery store*."

"I think you did," she said, smiling. "But I'm definitely not complaining. It looks delicious."

"But these are mere appetizers, *cara*. The main course still awaits within." Reaching into the cooler again, he withdrew a white cardboard box. "Lobsters," he said, savoring the word. "Fresh and succulent, ready for steaming."

"Fresh for—" Cat followed his gaze to the string-tied box where a faint scratching noise could be heard. "You mean they're in there? *Alive?*" she asked, biting her lower lip.

"Not for long," Diego assured her, producing a medium-size metal boiling pot and preparing to fire up the portable *camping* stove he'd packed. "Pirates are always prepared," he told her with a wink. "This is a recipe Scurvy taught me when I was no more than a brass monkey on a merchant ship, hired to keep the hardware polished to a perfect shine. A fresh-caught seafood specialty handed down from one old pirate to the next. You will surely love it, lass."

"Only if it's an old pirate you're planning to boil in there!" she exclaimed. "Stop!"

"Stop?" Diego turned toward her with a puzzled frown. "Do you not like seafood, sweet?"

She stepped up to the box and bent her head toward it until her ear was nearly level with its side. "Sure, I like it. As long as it's not still kicking. Listen to the poor little things trying to escape. Don't you hear them struggling? That's lobster code for 'Let me out!' "

"Squeamish?" Diego asked her, deciding there was still much to be learned about the unpredictable Catalina.

"Sympathetic," she responded. "Do we *have* to eat them?"

Diego shrugged. "What did you have in mind, *cara*? Would you prefer that I behead them more speedily with my sword? They will die quick and painless deaths at my hand, I promise."

"We *could* let them go," she offered, a little doubtful of his reaction.

"But, sweet, I have hardly brought anything else to eat . . ."

"I'd rather starve than send those two crustaceans to their deaths," she exclaimed, glaring at the metal steaming pot. "It's a horrible way to go."

Diego stared hard at Catalina as though she had come halfway unhinged. A lady with a soft heart for spiny sea creatures? The more time he spent with the unpredictable woman, the more intriguing she became, throwing his expectations completely off kilter. Once again, the lass had knocked him for a loop.

In fact, lunch wasn't progressing at all the way he'd planned. She should have been melting in his arms by now. Instead, she was more concerned about the pair of lobsters melting in their pot. It seemed he still had much to discover about the way the mind of his modern woman worked.

With deep regret, he lifted the white box and handed it to her. "Here. Follow me."

He led her to the side of the boat.

"You mean it?" she asked, looking up at him with questioning copper eyes.

"It is your lunch, lass," he answered solemnly, "and *mine*," he added, groaning. "If it is your wish to send *fifty dollars'* worth of delicious food scrambling back into the ocean, then I will grant it. But have some mercy, sweet, and do it now, before my protesting stomach causes me to change my mind."

She gave him a grateful smile, pulled open the lid, and upended the box. The lobsters did not take long to react. They pointed their antennae south and headed into the surf at top speed. Two seconds later, they were gone.

"It is a lucky thing I did not plan on escargot for appetizers," he said ruefully. "I have an inkling you'd be marching them off to the nearest shore before the butter even began to melt."

She grinned back at him. "Sorry for spoiling your nice meal. But don't you feel better?"

Diego tried to come to grips with exactly what he was feeling. Other than grievous disappointment, that is, at the thought of his favorite food cavorting gleefully away. Shock came next as he realized that there was nothing he wouldn't do for the woman beside him.

Nothing at all. And for a woman he had not even bedded! Never had a lady affected him so thoroughly.

But he had never known one of Catalina's kind before. She was willful and unyielding, tender and turbulent, an angel and a spitfire all rolled into one. The kind that could squirm with the strength of an octopus when she was angry, or kiss with the sweet, raw sensuality of a siren.

If he ever did manage to make love to her, she would set off an explosion inside him more volatile than cannon fire. The prospect of it pleased him to no end.

He had been bewitched by the auburn beauty, mesmerized by the gleaming copper eyes until he could no longer steer straight. Indeed, he was in love with Catalina.

He was sunk for certain.

Aye, and he suspected that Catalina cared for him as well. Had she not shown him how much by helping him to procure a new identity? It was a new experience for him to have a woman worry for his welfare. Plenty had professed their feelings for him, but it was not difficult to become enamored of a high-paying privateer after sharing a few fine hours with him. Silver and gold had a way of making all manner of wenches amazingly devoted to a man.

But Ms. Steadwell knew that he was no more than a pauper. Nay, she cared not a whit for his current state of poverty. She seemed to care for him, instead.

So what was he going to do about it?

Diego Swift would seduce her most thoroughly and be done with it. But Douglas Smith would attempt to do the honorable thing. What *was* the honorable thing, anyway?

"Time to shove off, lass," he told her, taking the wheel and firing up the engine before she took it into her head to throw the rest of their meal overboard. He had no doubt he would comply with that wish as well, if she were inclined to make it.

Steering out of the cove and north along the waterway, he took a smooth right turn toward the St. Augustine inlet, heading straight for open ocean. The wind whipped past him at a speed he would never have imagined possible were he not experiencing it for himself. But in spite of the accelerated pace, the sun and the sky and the stinging salt spray against his face were familiar. He had missed it, the freedom. He hadn't realized how much.

He looked back at Catalina. She had a taste for seafaring as well, it seemed. She was stretched out on the reclining chair, welcoming the wind in her hair, the sun on her fair skin. Welcoming it as much as he did.

He turned forward again, facing straight into the wind, and let the sun-swept breeze buffet him. But as fine as the freedom felt at the moment, as effortless and easy, he knew that the moment was fleeting. Diego, Douglas, it didn't matter. Either way, he was a free man no longer.

Catalina had already captured him.

He had been in this new age nearly a month now, and his prospects for returning to his own time looked slim. Nay, they looked next to impossible. There was little or no likelihood of yet another strange storm blowing him back again. But he would not take the opportunity to return there, even if it were possible.

He had no wish to go back. He had a longing to remain and live up to the promise of his fine, new name. Maybe he could make himself over into a *good guy* this time around and make a new life with the one woman who believed in him as no one else ever had.

Ms. Catalina Steadwell. Would she be willing to take that chance with him, throw her cautious side to the wind and start afresh?

Would she be willing to marry him in the eyes of God alone?

A tiny island was approaching on their starboard side, no more than a palm-and-pine-sheltered bump of sand half a mile or so from the peninsula's shore.

He guided the craft into a shallow shoal along the island's edge and dropped anchor.

"Oh!" Catalina exclaimed. "It's beautiful. A little piece of paradise."

Aye, Diego agreed silently. It was sweet heaven on earth there with her. At least it would be.

"Why are we stopping?" she asked. "Did you want to go for a swim?"

"Indeed, *cara*. But I have more in mind for us than that. There is a question I wish to ask you."

EIGHT

Cat could not for the life of her imagine what Diego's question was. She only knew he seemed determined not to ask it until later. At least until after their swim.

In spite of the burning curiosity his words had stirred inside her, she was determined not to miss out on the beauty of the moment at hand. The tiny island was lovelier than any she'd seen before, with sandy white beaches, swaying shady palms, and warm blue water lapping along the shell-strewn shore, beckoning them to sample the storybook serenity.

Cat didn't wait long before accepting the invitation. She hesitated only a shy moment or two before stripping her shorts off to the bikini bottoms beneath and making a beeline for the glittering water.

"Come on!" she called to Diego, lowering herself over the side of the boat and plunging feetfirst into the sandy-bottomed shallows. "Last one in is a slimy sea serpent."

The water was deliciously warm, but still several degrees cooler than the ambient air, drenching her sun-kissed skin with liquid refreshment. The tide was dropping, bringing the water level to a height just above her waist. Cat shook her hair loose from its restraining bun, took a deep breath, and ducked the rest of her body beneath the waves.

Diego caught her in his arms as she surfaced.

"A sea serpent, am I, sweet?" he purred dangerously, wrapping his long, suntanned fingers around her waist. "Perhaps the kind that snatches maidens from the beach and spirits them away to a secluded, undersea lair?"

"Helpless maidens," she corrected him, splashing a handful of water in his face with her free arm and making a successful escape to a spot several feet away. "Which I am not!"

"Nay!" he laughed, wiping the salty droplets from his eyes with a single swipe of one well-muscled arm. "You have never been helpless around me, Catalina. No matter how much I might wish to make you so. Helpless to resist me, that is."

Catalina's heart tumbled over at the words. If he only knew, she thought silently. He might've had her on the first night he'd met her if he'd wanted to. She *was* helpless around a man of his size. Physically at his mercy, that is.

No woman would stand a chance against him if he tried to take what he wanted by force. But that wasn't the kind of helpless he was talking about. Diego didn't merely want her physical surrender.

He wanted her emotional surrender as well. *He wanted all of her.*

Cat's breathing quickened painfully as she became aware of how alone they were at this moment. How isolated from the rest of the world. The little quay and the waters that surrounded it were completely deserted. Was there a reason he'd brought her there, where they were so perfectly protected from any outside intrusion?

What was it he wanted to ask of her?

Whatever it was, she wasn't sure she'd have the strength to refuse. Not now. Not here.

Not him.

She drank in the sunlit sight of him. He tossed his head back, flicking the excess water from his sleek jet hair and burnished bronze shoulders. The droplets streamed down across his torso like a sheet of rippling transparent silk, highlighting hard muscles and dark, dripping body hair, returning to the ocean again in a slick, shimmering cascade around his narrow, suit-clad hips.

His thumbs were hooked in the waistline of his swim trunks, dragging the beltline a few inches lower than where it belonged. Cat could see the top of his tan line and the contrasting swath of paler skin just below. The image was raw, sensual, and shockingly exciting.

"You're staring, lass."

"What?" The sound of his voice brought her out

of her reverie. Fast. "No, I was just . . ." Mercy, she *had* been staring. Or more accurately, she'd been *gawking*. At his crotch no less, and he *knew* it. What had come over her?

"Enjoying the view?" he supplied, grinning.

Cat felt her face growing hot with embarrassment. Never in her life had she behaved so shamelessly. Was it the Madeira that had affected her, or was it the man?

She pretended to study the picturesque horizon and the stunning scenery beyond. "Uh-huh."

"It is nothing to be ashamed of, sweet. Curiosity is entirely natural." His eyes flared to a brilliant blue as he studied her openly. "As is my own interest."

Interest? The way he was sizing her up with his eyes was more than that. It was urgent.

His stare was focused for the moment on her suit top, the small stretchy scrap they'd discussed before. What was it he still found so fascinating about it? A quick glance down at the garment brought Cat her answer.

The water had wrought an amazing change.

Where it had been dry before, and only slightly skimpy, now it was wet. And clinging. And see-through!

Everything was visible, from the edge of her tan line to the rosy-red circles at the center of her breasts where her nipples strained tautly against the cool, wet fabric. She might as well have been naked, for all the shocking sexual details that were showing. No, this was worse than being naked. It was brazen.

She was *aroused*, for heaven's sake, and he hadn't even touched her. Her own body had betrayed her, revealing how much she wanted him. For Cat, it was almost painful to show so much of herself to Diego. There was no cloak of darkness to protect her now, no sheets to draw up around her body, barring his hot, blue gaze. There was only the lush, steaming air, the tropical sun, and the water swirling gently around them. She put a hand up to her forehead, hiding her face.

"Do not turn away from me, *cara*," he said hoarsely, catching her by the arm and tipping her face up until their eyes met. "It is nothing I have not seen before. Seen and enjoyed. You are so beautiful, sweet. *This*," he said, glancing down at the full, over-flowing outline of her breasts, and brushing his long fingertips across the hardened buds of her nipples, "is beautiful. The way you respond to me."

Cat gasped as the vibrant sensation lanced through her, so intensely pleasurable, it was almost pain. But Diego didn't let up on her. He took her hand in his, guiding it toward the spot she'd been staring at only minutes before. The upper edge of his swimming trunks and the dangerous, forbidden hardness below.

Gently, he touched her fingertips to it. "So you may know how *I* respond to you, *cara*."

Cat's heart went a little wild. She had never touched a man's hardness before, not even in her single, somewhat disappointing sexual encounter at the age of sixteen.

Diego was more than massive. He was all rampant, rock-hard energy, all stiff, straining male muscle. He was aroused. Incredibly so. Lord, was that what she did to him?

She gave him a soft stroke, testing, and felt his entire body shudder in response.

"Easy, sweet," he groaned roughly, pulling her hand away. "That is a stick of gunpowder you are playing with."

He wasn't kidding, Cat thought. He was a lit keg of dynamite, ready to go off.

Inside her.

No, she couldn't even *think* about the possibility of that. But Diego's condition did make her realize what holding himself back had cost him. Plenty.

The other night in his attic bedroom, he'd stopped himself for her sake. He might not know how to play by all the modern rules, or for that matter, even care to, but what greater act of chivalry was there than putting her own feelings above his?

"Do you understand now how much I would like to make love to you, lass?"

"Yes." And she did. Graphically. "But I thought you understood how I feel about all that. I'm just not capable of a physical relationship without a long-term commitment."

"Aye, but in spite of that, sweet, I cannot keep my body from responding. I am not what you would call a *superman.*"

She gave him a quick, shy smile. "Don't be so sure about that, Captain."

"I am sure of nothing where you are concerned, *cara*. Except this—" He caught her by the waist, took her chin in his hand again and held her gaze hard, staring deep into her eyes. "I wish to marry you."

If he hadn't been holding her upright, Cat's legs would've given way beneath her. She'd never, ever expected to hear those words from Diego Swift. She'd never even dared to dream them.

"Was—was that why you brought me here?" she asked, her voice no more than a soft, stunned whisper. "To propose?"

Come to think of it, he hadn't actually proposed. He'd made a simple, commanding statement. *I wish to marry you.* But then, pirates probably weren't used to going down on their knees in front of trembling, bikini-clad wenches and asking them to be their wives. Very likely, that sort of wildly romantic gesture would be seriously frowned upon in the swashbuckler's book of rules. From a man like Diego, the admission itself was enough.

"Aye, Catalina. Proposing to you was my intention. Although I had planned to make a better job of it. I was distracted by you, lass, and the words took me unawares." He scooped her up in his arms and carried her to the island's shore, setting her down gently on the soft, pristine sand at the water's edge. Dropping to his knees in front of her, he took her hand in his. "Will you marry me, Catalina?"

Cat felt her throat go tight at the sound of those strong, sexy, incredibly wondrous words. It seemed Diego did know the proper way to propose after all.

He had made a major decision in his life and had chosen to throw his roving pirate past to the wind. He had chosen to settle down with her, instead.

He wanted to marry her!

Staring down into his sunlit gaze, Cat knew his intentions were one-hundred-percent sincere. Those incredible eyes of his said what his smooth, chivalrous words could not. They seemed to take possession of her with a single glance, penetrating her heart, her soul, searching for the only response that Diego wanted to hear.

Yes.

It was an answer Cat wasn't sure she could give. How could she say yes when so many obstacles still seemed to block any possible union between them? Two hundred years' worth of obstacles. They came from different times, different worlds. Diego seemed to be adjusting gradually to this one, but would they really be able to overcome all the complications?

Would he truly be able to put his past behind him and give up his wandering ways?

"Diego," she said, "are you sure you know what you're asking? Not only of me, but of yourself?"

He continued staring up at her, his expression certain, serious. "I would never ask such a question lightly, lass."

Cat took in a deep breath and letting it out slowly, determined to make him see exactly what marriage meant to her. What it would also have to mean to him. "We would be bound to each other," she said. "For life. Forever. You would be *leg-shackled*."

"Aye," he agreed. "Happily so."

"No more roving," she added. "No more carousing with *chicks* at the corner bar. No more sailing off at the spur of the moment."

He brought her hand to his lips and kissed it. "I care naught for any of that, *cara*. I only care for you."

Cat sighed heavily, feeling herself weakening, wondering if she was actually losing the battle or winning it. Now that Diego would be assuming the identity of Douglas Smith, their marriage could be legally recognized. She could finally have what she'd longed for all her life. The security of truly belonging to someone and having that someone belong to her.

But was Diego really ready for that kind of commitment? Was he trying to make too many changes in his new life all at once?

"Say yes," he prompted, "and I will do all that is in my power to make you happy, *cara*. You have given me reason to live again. You have given me hope. Say yes, and the future is ours."

The future. It was the one thing they had in common. The one thing they could hold on to, in spite of the past and present differences between them. She had encouraged him to take hold of his own future, and make it into what he wanted. Wasn't it about time she took some of her own advice and did the same for herself?

Diego had the courage to change. Did she? Was

there enough spirit left in her to overcome her cautious side and go with her gut feeling?

"Yes," she whispered, smiling down at him as tears filled her eyes. "I will."

He was kissing her hand then, cradling it against his face as though he would never let go. He was on his feet again, lifting her up, carrying her across the shallow waves back toward the boat.

"Wait!" she exclaimed, laughter bubbling up inside her as buoyantly as the happiness that was beginning to take hold of her heart. "Where are we going? We just got here!"

"We are going to get married!" Diego told her.

"Now?" she asked, still in a state of ecstatic, overjoyed shock. "Don't you think we should at least wait until we've had a late lunch?"

"Nay," he said firmly. "I see no reason to wait one moment longer to wed you. Now is as fine a time as any to accomplish the ceremony, sweet."

"You're serious! You really do mean now, as in *now*, this second?"

"Aye," he agreed, helping her up the ladder of the powerboat and following her over the swaying side and onto the deck again. "It may be a while before we are out on a boat again, and I have it in my mind to perform the ceremony myself. Sea captains, you see, have the authority to conduct marriages on a ship they are in command of."

"Even pirate captains?" Cat teased, secretly finding the idea of it incredibly romantic and terrifying at the same time. How could she let herself go along with such a crazy, impulsive idea?

"Especially pirate captains," he assured her, flashing a wide white grin. "Ours is not the sort of authority most men have the inclination to question."

"I see your point," she answered, laughing. "But, Diego, I'm not sure . . . we don't have a license. It won't be legal. Don't you think we should wait a couple of weeks until your birth certificate shows up?"

"Nay," he told her. "I do not. I wish to make my promises to you now, Catalina, while they are strong in my heart. Of course, we will apply for a license at the first opportunity, but in the meanwhile we can say our vows to each other, with the Lord above as our audience. I cannot imagine a more joyous and solemn ceremony than that."

Come to think of it, Cat couldn't either. The license itself would be the only thing missing, and it wouldn't be long before they could be granted one by the state. Still, the sensible thing to do would be to wait until all the documents and details were in order. But it was the lack of that little piece of paper, a marriage license, that had created so much childhood misery for her. Was she going to let it ruin this marvelous moment in her life as well?

"Legal documents do not define love," Diego added, as if reading her mind. "Men and women do that."

"Do you realize what you're asking of me?" she pleaded.

"Aye," he said calmly. "I am asking you to trust me."

She let out a long, heartfelt sigh. "This will be your last act as a captain," she said, reminding him of the commitment she expected in return for that trust. "Once we're married, there's no going back to that way of life."

"Then a fitting end to my career it will be, lass. Maybe the only truly good thing that ever came of it."

His career, Cat thought. A way of life that had been full of chances and uncertainty. If there was one thing she'd learned from Diego Swift, it was how to take a risk. And this was a big one. But somewhere deep inside, she knew it was right.

Her decision had been made. Maybe it was the most reckless, daring, hotheaded thing she'd ever done in her life, but that was the real thrill of it. For once, the cautious, careful, convent-reared Catalina Steadwell was plunging into life, headfirst, without a safety net.

"Just give me a minute," she said, slipping her cover-up on again and running a comb through her long, wet hair.

Getting married in a bikini was a little too daring. No matter how impulsive the moment was, Cat knew it was nothing to take lightly. She believed in the institution of marriage, from the bottom of her heart. She could only pray that Diego understood the gravity of what they were about to do. She could only hope that his commitment to their future was as deep and certain as hers.

The ceremony was as brief and beautiful as the summer day around them. The waves lapping gently against the side of the boat made music as they stood together in the bow, promising to love, honor, and cherish each other for a lifetime. Diego even had a ring to give her—an intricate sailor's knot, tied from narrow lengths of twine into a delicate, beautifully braided circular design.

"It is no fine jewel of the sort I would prefer to bestow upon you," he said, "but merely a small gift I have been weaving at night in the attic. Many mariners make such things to pass the time at sea. Sailor's valentines they used to call them."

"It's lovely," Cat exclaimed as he slipped it on her finger. She loved it all the more because he'd made it for her himself.

"We are husband and wife now, Catalina," he said, bending to kiss her. "We belong to each other."

Cat melted against him, ready to burst from happiness. And excitement. With no audience to watch the postnuptial kiss, Diego apparently saw no reason to make it a tame one.

It was the deepest, most possessive kiss he'd ever given her. So hot and searing, Cat felt as though she'd been beautifully branded by it. He stole inside her with the sweet, heavy battering of his tongue and left her weak with wanting for him. With that one kiss he left his taste in her mouth, his scent on her body, a territorial male marking that said he meant to claim her for his own.

Very soon.

Cat hardly had a moment to savor the bliss of her wedding day before she realized what would undoubtedly follow.

The wedding night.

She'd almost forgotten that minor detail in the madness of the last hour. But Diego had effectively reminded her of it with the kiss. Cat felt a sharp thrill at the thought. A thrill of fear as she remembered how he'd felt against her fingertips.

Massive.

Cat broke the kiss prematurely, feeling overwhelmed by it all, and suddenly shy. "We should celebrate," she suggested, her eyes lighting on the cooler and realizing that a slow, afternoon bread-and-cheese feast would give her at least an hour or two's reprieve. "How about a postwedding picnic on that beautiful beach over there?"

"If you wish, lass, although I am strangely not hungry any longer."

Could've fooled me, she thought silently, noting that Diego's eyes were fairly burning with hunger. If looks could devour, he would've just eaten her alive.

"I think we definitely need some food," she told him seriously.

"Of course, *cara*, you may be right. Some nourishment will go a long way to build up our strength."

Cat swallowed at the comment, grabbing her straw beach bag, climbing down out of the boat again

and motioning for Diego to follow. The last thing a
man of his size and apparent endurance needed was
more strength. For heaven's sake, he was already
built up enough!

Unfortunately, her brilliant plan to eat took only
a fraction of the time she'd hoped for. Their food
was delicious, the fresh fruit divine, but there was a
limit to the amount of bread and Brie you could eat
on a stomach that was already full of butterflies.

Diego stretched himself out beside her on the
beach blanket, toying with the long, drying tendrils
of her hair. "I believe I like being married, lass."

"Oh?"

"Indeed. I may touch you now and know that it is
within my rights to do so. In fact, it is a state that
gives me not less freedom, but more."

"Well—" Cat had never looked at it in quite that
way. "Yes, I—see what you mean." And she did. She
hadn't just plighted her troth to this man. She'd
given him a license to do almost anything to her,
including making wild, abandoned love!

"What we do from now on is no sin in the eyes of
heaven," Diego continued, seeming to carefully consider all the fascinating new aspects of their current
married state. "In fact, it is our conjugal duty to pleasure each other to the limits, is it not?"

"To the limits?" she breathed, trying to imagine
just how far those limits might be from a swashbuckler's experienced perspective. "I—suppose." The
state of *wedded bliss* had just taken on a whole new
meaning.

"This island is entirely deserted, Catalina."

"Oh? Are you sure? I mean, some other boaters *could* come along."

"Nay, not without our hearing them long before."

"Oh."

"We could swim bare in the ocean if we wanted to, and there would be no one around to see us."

"Naked?" Cat asked, gasping softly. "Well, that does sound, uh—very sensual, but—you see, I have such fair skin, I might—sunburn."

"Indeed, we would not want this soft skin of yours to burn," he said hoarsely, running his long, caressing fingers down the length of her bare arms. "But is that not what your bottle of *sunscreen* is for?" he asked, indicating the telltale tube that was easily visible in the wide open pouch of her beach bag. "In fact, I feel it is my husbandly duty to rub some on you right now."

"Thanks, but—"

"Lie back, Catalina," he said, unscrewing the cap and squirting a handful of the creamy white stuff onto his open palm. "This will not hurt a bit."

"Well . . ."

Catching the hem of her baggy cover-up with the other hand, he gave a quick tug upward and had her stripped nearly to the flesh again in seconds. "Lie back," he repeated sternly and positioned her carefully on her stomach.

The lotion was cool on her shoulders when he began to rub her there, cool and rich and so relaxing, she hardly had the opportunity to focus on anything else except the slow, steady movements of his hands. The taut muscles of her back began to lose their tension under his expert ministrations, flowing into a languorous, dreamy state as thick and sensual as the liquid he was working into them. Magic fingers, Cat thought, sinking into the soft beach blanket and the gentle cushion of sand beneath. The man was an artist.

But just as she was starting to grow all soft and mellow from the warmth of his hands, they moved lower on her body. Much lower.

"We would not want your legs to become sunburned, Catalina," Diego told her, working his way down along the curve of one bare calf and gradually up the tingling length of the other.

A sigh welled in Catalina's throat. It felt good to have him touch her there. So good. But then those magic fingers were on the move again, traveling all the way up to the top of her legs, to the tender dimple of skin that met the edge of her bathing suit bottom. She gasped and her muscles tensed with excitement.

Diego continued stroking, rubbing, massaging until the tops of her thighs were so well protected from the sun, they were slick and wet from being slathered with lotion. But it wasn't just the outside of Cat's body that was affected by all the attention. Her stomach was taut with a shivering vibrancy unlike any sensation she'd ever experienced before.

Desire? Longing? She wasn't sure, but suddenly

she wasn't so afraid. She wanted him. Not just there, along the trembling tops of her legs, but everywhere.

She flipped onto her back, exposing the front of her body to his view. And to his amazing hands. Diego didn't have to ask. The sexy glow in his eyes told her he understood perfectly. He knew exactly what she wanted. What she needed.

More lotion.

He squeezed a long, narrow strip of it out of the tube and across the flat surface of her stomach. Cat's breath caught as he began to work it in, starting in a wide circle that swept from just beneath her swimsuit top to just above the hipline of her bikini bottom. The circle narrowed, dropping to smaller and smaller concentric rings until his fingers were concentrating entirely on a small, vulnerable spot just a few inches below her belly button. A spot that led straight down to the narrow vee of her pelvic bone and the gently throbbing cleft of female flesh that crowned her inner thighs.

His fingers darted, retreated, coaxed, caressed, but never quite touched her there, where she was already aroused for him. Lord, but she *wanted* him to touch her there, the ache inside her was that strong. But he wasn't ready yet. He seemed to be enjoying the teasing too much.

"Diego," Cat whispered, struggling for air, "you're torturing me."

"Aye, lass," he agreed hoarsely, "and you are returning the favor. Now strip your brassiere away for me because I intend to torture you much more before we are through."

"My top?" she whispered, going weak at the thought of what he intended to do to her naked breasts. "Please," she moaned. "I can't. I don't think I can take it."

"*Cara,*" he whispered back, bending over her to rain tender kisses across her flushed face. "I will stop anytime you ask me to. Now, if that is your wish. *Is* that your wish, sweet?"

Cat knew that if he did stop now she would probably be weeping with regret instead of gasping from unfulfilled sexual need. But it was more than mere need she felt for him. It was emotional desire as well. The desire to make the most beautiful love imaginable to the only man she loved. It was welling so strongly inside her, she knew she had to have him.

All of him.

"No," she moaned softly. "I don't want you to stop."

"Then strip your top away, sweet," he commanded, his own voice urgent with need, "unless you would prefer me to do it for you."

With shaking hands, Cat complied. The fabric slid, gradually giving way until her breasts were bare before him.

Diego wondered if his heart would survive a night with this woman, so strong was it hammering against his chest. But when she finally pulled her brassiere away, it very nearly stopped. He could not for the life of him imagine what he had done to deserve Catalina for his wife. So sweet she was, so responsive to his every move, as if the heavens had made them for each other.

Her breasts shimmered, round and full, straining for his touch. Diego swore to himself that he would touch them, every velvet inch of them. Nay, he would taste them, so strong was his hunger for Catalina.

He did both, cupping one with his hand, massaging the cresting center as he took the second swollen peak into his mouth, nipping gently, tugging and suckling at the sweet round bud until she writhed against him, slick with lotion, warm with naked, wet need. He pulled again on the delicate tip, drinking deeply with his lips, rubbing his teeth ever so lightly against the engorged edges of her nipple.

She whimpered softly, calling out his name. The sound of it on her lips made his body tighten in fierce, rock-hard response. Never had he grown this hard for a woman, but then never had he made love to his wife before. He drew back for a moment, knowing he would never last as long as he desired to if she continued to cry for him so sweetly.

He returned to the lotion instead, understanding that another form of pleasure would suffice for a time, yet keep them both hovering just below an explosive peak. Rubbing a ribbon of the silken cream between his hands, he returned his attention to her breasts, working the lotion slowly into each pliant mound, steering his fingers clear of the pebbled centers. But even this form of kinder ravishment brought his *cara* little relief.

In seconds, she was begging him to taste her again, his careful ministrations only seeming to have made her need that much stronger. Diego himself could not resist such an urgent invitation. He used the full length of his tongue this time, lathing it across the peaking pink aureoles in long, slow, languid strokes. Cat raked her short nails across the top of his back, sending his own pleasure soaring.

"Please, Diego," she whispered wildly against him, "I'm ready."

He caught her up in his arms, hugging her tight. "Hang on for me awhile longer, lass. I wish to make this time as memorable for you as I might."

Memorable? It already was that. The need he was eliciting within her was far too powerful to ever forget. But it was the bear-size hug he'd just given her that was really doing crazy things to the tenderest muscle in her body.

Her heart.

It expanded, swelling with the overwhelming surge of emotion she felt for him. He was so *kind*. Not at all the wild, careless lover that history had made him out to be.

"You really do care for me," she said.

He drew back to look at her, his eyes dark and heavy with desire. "What were you expecting, sweet? A scoundrel who would take you at the first opportunity?"

"I—didn't know. I had no idea you could hold

yourself back so long—for my sake. Does it hurt?" she asked him shyly.

"It is *torture*," he said, flashing her a disarming grin. "But the kind I do not mind at all."

"Sweet torture," Cat agreed, sighing.

"Come into the water with me, *cara*," he said, scooping her up in his arms and carrying her to the ocean's edge. "It will cool us off."

Cat didn't think so. Especially when she saw what kind of swimming Diego had in mind. He waded into the waist-high basin just a few feet beyond the beach and eased her down in front of him. With the same disregard for nudity he'd shown from the start, he began to strip off his shorts.

Cat made a small, shocked sound. "Diego . . ."

"Modest, Catalina? I am not. For your sake, however . . ." He turned his back on her, completing the process with at least a modicum of decency.

Cat swallowed hard as he tossed the bright swim trunks back onto the beach. That was when she noticed it. The tattoo. The one she'd seen that first night and never really gotten a good look at.

She looked at it now, realizing that it wasn't the crude or macho sort of sailor's decoration she'd been expecting. It was beautiful. A sleek black bird of some sort with wide, outstretched wings, a sharply scissored tail and a brilliant slash of red at its throat. Enchanted by the wild image, Cat put her hand out to touch it.

Diego shuddered in response, stilled.

"It's gorgeous," Cat commented. "What is it?"

"A frigate bird," he said. "A tropical seabird from the southern islands that soars like the wind. I will take you there someday, *cara*, so you may see them for yourself." He turned around to face her again. "Meanwhile . . ."

Meanwhile, there were other fascinating sights for Cat to take in. Strangely thrilling sights. The wet, wild-looking pirate standing in front of her, for instance. Perfectly naked.

Perfectly *built*.

In spite of her sudden shyness, Cat couldn't bring herself to turn away. He was sunk in water nearly to his hips but still exposed, from the black velvet vee of swirling body hair to the erotic view of his arousal, clearly visible just beneath the lightly lapping waves.

Her breath caught, seeming to stall somewhere deep in her throat. Moments before, Cat had imagined she was ready. Now, she wasn't so sure.

"You must take your turn now," he told her. "Much as I admire your *bikini*, I would ask you to remove it. Please, Catalina. All of it."

Diego had come a long way with his modern manners, Cat realized. He had learned to be so courteous, so civil. He had learned how to coax her to strip for him, just by asking! What a polite scoundrel her new husband was.

Still, she trusted him entirely. With her body, her life. She took a leap of faith, believing in him completely.

Reaching into the water, she tugged at the waistband of her suit bottom, and peeled the final shred of her clothing away. Tossing it onto the beach with a reckless abandon she could barely believe, she stood before Diego, naked.

"*Make* me ready," she said, and moved toward him.

NINE

Diego held himself back with an effort, checking the almost irresistible impulse to carry Cat back onto the beach, lay her down against the hot sand and bury himself inside her. Never had his urge to bed a woman been so strong.

Aye, he had wanted women before, but the bare beauty before him made them all pale in pitiful comparison. He had imagined it would take several minutes of coaxing to get those skimpy bikini bottoms off Catalina. It had only taken one.

The lass was blessedly willing. Nay, she was more impetuous than that. That tortuous maneuver with her bathing suit, where she'd tossed it so provocatively onto the beach, had been as pleasurable for her as it was for him. She was finding her freedom at last.

And tempting him unmercifully in the process.

His sweet was killing him slowly. Before he had a chance to recover his breath at her fully naked beauty, she was pressing the length of her lithe body against him, teasing, tempting, urging him to plunder her.

Diego wasted no time in obliging her.

He palmed the back of her buttocks with his wet hands, pressing her still closer against him, making her physically aware of his hardness.

"Oh!" She gave a startled gasp.

"Easy, lass," he responded, massaging her bottom, soothing her sweetly. "Do not be afraid. Give yourself a moment to imagine how our bodies will fit."

It seemed Cat was imagining, quite vividly. Instead of moving away from him in fear, she eased closer, beginning to sway her lower body instinctively, rhythmically, and creating a friction between them that set him aflame. Afraid? He was the one who should be in fear. For his own sanity. The woman was driving him to distraction.

What wild, amazing thing would she do to him next?

Diego did not wait to find out. He continued to hold her to him with one hand while he reached inside the water and began to plumb her tight, tender depths with the other. He found the most sensitive spot in seconds. The spot where she was slick and exquisitely responsive to his touch, so quiveringly responsive that the slightest stroke of his fingertips was enough to send her soaring.

He did more than stroke her there. He swept his fingers back and forth across it in full, insistent urgency, wanting her to feel just a little of the sweet, searing agony beginning to wrack his own body. Her soft cries sent a violent bolt of heat straight to his groin.

"Gracious," she gasped, the word so plaintive, it was almost a whimper, "that feels . . . incredible."

The woman was built to make love to a man, designed to give him nothing but pleasure. But Cat's clear enjoyment of the process made Diego's own experience that much more urgently sensual. It was nearly enough for him to take his own pleasure simply by giving Catalina hers.

Nearly.

He was aching to sample his woman's innermost secrets. Nothing short of claiming her fully would satisfy the conquering force that beat fiercely in his blood, blotting out everything except the sultry, smoldering heat of her sexuality.

Catalina stifled a gasp of pleasure as Diego's slowly stroking fingers began to probe her deeper, exploring, retreating, but always coming back to that aching, throbbing spot where her need for him was strongest. It was tender and swollen from the constant, circling friction he was applying, slick and moist, melting with desire. Her legs spread instinctively when he caressed her there, inviting him to go still deeper.

"Please," she begged, almost wild from the hot, crazy havoc that his hands were wreaking on her, "I need you soon, very soon. Diego, *please.*"

He inserted his fingers inside her then, thrusting

into the soft satin opening that flexed and fluttered, straining to accommodate him. "Tell me how much, *cara*," he said, penetrating the very depths of her being with his skillful, stroking touch, "I want to hear you say it."

Cat moaned in response, a sound that broke from somewhere deep within her. She was melting inside, going soft where he was touching her. The thrusting strokes of his fingers vibrated to the core of her, thrumming her body with music as sweet and vibrant as the taut, sultry strings of a Spanish guitar.

"Diego," she breathed. "I want you. I think I'm going to die if I don't have you. Now."

He carried her back to the beach then, laying her down on the blanket. "I can refuse you nothing, lass."

Cat gazed up at him in anticipation. Staring into his eyes, she saw a tenderness that nearly took her breath away. Her pirate wanted to please her, she realized, her heart constricting with emotion. The rugged, rakish scoundrel who had fenced and fought and plundered his way into history had stolen his way into her heart.

"Now?" she implored. "You really are going to make love to me right now?"

"I am going to make love to you, lass, until you can no longer move," he promised, positioning himself above her on the blanket, gently parting her knees with his own. "Nay, *we* are going to make mad, passionate love until the sun comes up."

Cat felt her heartbeat accelerate with every wild,

forbidden pirate's pleasure he promised her. And then she felt him spread her legs and press his hardness to that hot spot at the apex of her thighs, the place where she ached for him, yearned for him. A pulse beat in her throat, throbbing all the way down to the cleft of her legs, where she squirmed against him, swollen and pulsating with anticipation.

Muscles pulled tight deep inside her. She was frantic with need, more aroused with every exquisitely slow moment he made her wait. He pressed himself closer, touching his very tip to her slick, satin entrance, making full, frontal contact, but still holding himself back.

Cat strained upward instinctively, her whole body begging to feel the full length of him. He rotated his hips in response, making small, battering circles at the edges of her nerve-rich opening, tenderly pounding and probing until the teasing stimulation was too much for either of them.

Just when Cat thought he'd never take her, he did.

He entered her slowly, ever so slowly. Cat thought she was coming apart.

With ecstasy.

Diego's hardness was shattering her with pleasure, one gradual, mind-melting, heart-stopping inch at a time. It seemed a sweet, agonizing hour before he'd possessed her fully, sinking himself to the hilt in her heat. Cat arched beneath him, moaning softly as the peaks of her breasts grazed against him.

The motion seemed to incite him instinctively.

He withdrew himself halfway and plunged again inside her, thrusting to the very limits this time. Cat's head fell back as she gasped at the primitive, searing sensation, the most thrilling pleasure she had ever known. He rocked back again, pulling partway out of her, positioning his hands at the base of her bottom so her body could accommodate even more of him.

His thrust was so hard and deep, Cat felt her world begin to give way. She was climaxing like crazy before it was finished. She cried his name in wonderment, her eyes tearing with joy as the shuddering waves washed over her.

When Diego sensed she was peaking, he caught her up in his arms, whispering wild, abandoned words in her ear. The sight of her response was enough to send him over the edge. She was an irresistible siren in his arms, a vixen in the throes of some sweet, endless rapture that their loving had brought her to. He plunged inside her again, rocking and straining, seeking her depths with a fierce brand of passion he had never known before. He thrust again, one final time, one last enflamed moment before giving himself over to the overwhelming power of his own convulsive climax.

Indeed, it was the most explosive peak he had ever known. Aye, he had finally claimed his Catalina, but she had claimed him right back.

His body no longer belonged to him. She alone belonged to him. And he to her.

He dropped down on the sand beside her, holding her close.

Cat sighed, wondering if it was fair for any woman on earth to feel so happy. So satiated. It was all so perfect.

Well, *nearly* perfect. Diego's lovemaking had been incredible, satisfying her in ways that went beyond her wildest expectations. There was only one little thing she'd expected from him that he hadn't done, yet.

He hadn't told her that he loved her.

She'd been so worried about all the other issues confronting them that she'd simply assumed . . .

But of course, he loved her. Didn't he?

After all, he'd married her. More or less. At least, they would be *officially* married as soon as the birth certificate arrived.

Wouldn't they?

The sun was beginning to drop along the western edges of the islet when they were finally ready to leave. Catalina turned back, drinking in the seductive scenery, trying to embed the image in her memory forever. Banishing all of her foolish worries to the back of her mind, she was determined to forget her insecurities for the moment and simply enjoy the view.

The sky was turning fuchsia and purple, with red and rosy streaks along the edges like some voluptuous tropical blossom unfolding before her eyes.

Feathery white egrets were returning to their roosts to rest for the night, settling silently into the trees above them like a flock of ethereal angels, serene and hauntingly beautiful in the fading light. The beach itself had turned to dusty pink, and the ocean was a wild, constantly changing watercolor.

She squeezed her eyes shut, committing every gorgeous multihued detail of the special place to her memory as the boat sped away. It was a lush, exotic, perfect picture she would never forget.

"We are headed for home, now, wife," Diego reminded her, seeming to sense her slight, lingering sadness about leaving such an idyllic place and having to face the real world again. "Our home," he added, then flashed her a sudden grin. "I must admit I am looking well forward to sleeping in my own bed again, sweet. And I do *not* mean that bloody, uncomfortable, cramped excuse for a cot. I am far too old to be bedding down on such a bag of bones as that."

"Old?" Cat repeated. "You're hardly over the hill, Captain. And, I might add, in remarkable shape. Yes, definitely remarkable."

"Thank you for the compliment, lass, but you must remember I am well over two hundred years old!"

Cat crossed her arms in front of her and shot him a skeptical smile. "I see what you mean. In fact, you must be quite feeble and infirm."

"Aye. I will require a great deal of bed rest. And perhaps a private nurse to see to my every need."

"An expensive proposition," she told him. "Too bad we're too poor to hire someone for the job."

"Nay," he said, smiling. "I already have someone in mind. Someone whose needs I will be happy to see to in return."

"I can't tell you how glad I am to hear you say that," Cat answered with a sly, provocative smile. "There are any number of odd jobs around the house that still need doing. Painting, carpentry, floor refinishing. And that poor plumber you almost strangled never has come back, you know."

"You are merciless, *cara*," he commented. "Perhaps we should consider hiring someone for all these dull jobs."

Her eyebrows lifted in surprise. "Really? Are you thinking about getting a different job?"

"Something like that," he told her, rubbing the dark, sandpaper stubble that was beginning to form along his chin and jawline. "Now that I will be getting a Social Security number, it might be possible to find some sort of employment where my skills are better suited. But let us not worry about those details right now. My mind is currently occupied with other ideas. Like getting back home and bedding you properly. In our own bed."

Gracious, Cat thought, was he ready again, already? Not that she was complaining. But for a two-hundred-year-old man, he did have an amazing amount of energy.

When they finally did make it back into their bed

later that night, Diego postponed the lovemaking for a while in order to give her a gift.

"A wedding present," he said, handing her a small, rather poorly wrapped package.

"Oh!"

Cat was touched to her core by the unexpected gesture. It didn't even matter to her what was in the plain little box. It only mattered that he had given it to her. She lifted the lid, her throat constricting with emotion when she saw what was nestled in the small tuft of cotton. A lovely pink seashell.

"From the beach today," he explained. "To wear as a necklace, lass, as soon as I can procure you a chain. You see, there is already a small hole in it."

"Yes," Catalina said, breaking into tears, "I see."

"Do not cry, Catalina," he commanded. "I can not bear for you to cry. It is not such a fine gift, anyway. I would prefer to shower you with pearls. Someday," he promised, "I will."

"It's beautiful," she told him. "Thank you."

She leaned forward in bed to kiss him. Now was the time, she told herself, to bring up that one small issue that had been nagging at her. The words she'd wanted to hear back at the beach that still remained unspoken.

At the moment, Cat felt close enough to Diego to tell him anything. But before she could get the question out, a sound came wafting up to them from the first floor below. A strong, insistent pounding against the front door.

"Visitors?" she asked, frowning, reaching for her robe. "At this hour?"

Diego went downstairs to check. Cat heard the door fly open. There was a moment of stunned, absolute silence, and then all hell broke loose.

At least it sounded like hell to Catalina, so loud were the shouts and hails and hollers floating up to her from the foyer below.

"Scurvy!" Diego yelled.

"Captain!" a man's voice bellowed back.

"Scurvy, old man, you are alive!"

"Captain, you young scoundrel of a sea dog, so are the likes of you!"

Catalina rushed to the top of the staircase just in time to witness a round of friendly slapping and chucking and generally cordial male bonding rituals that she didn't entirely understand. The two were old friends, that much was apparent. And judging by the looks of the older man and the description she'd had of him from Diego, there was only one person it could be.

Mr. Scurvy, Diego's first mate from the *Mystress*. He wasn't dead after all. It seemed he had been tossed forward in time, as well.

"Mate," Diego said fondly, "I thought for sure you had drowned."

"Nay, nay," Scurvy responded. "I was waylaid for a while is all. An adventure of the most amazing sort is what I have witnessed these past weeks. Break out a bit of rum, Captain, and pull up a chair. I have much to relate."

Diego glanced up, apparently remembering Cat's presence in the house. "Old friend," he said, glancing back at Scurvy. "There is someone I want you to meet."

The old man looked up at her on the landing in suspicious confusion.

With an uneasy feeling of impending doom, Cat plastered her friendliest smile across her slightly sunburned face and walked down the staircase to meet them.

"Catalina," Diego said, holding out his hand for her. "Mr. Scurvy is alive and well. You will remember we spoke of him?"

She nodded politely.

"Now then, Mr. Scurvy," he continued, "this is Ms. Catalina Steadwell. The house we are in is half hers."

"Hers!" Scurvy exclaimed indignantly. "How can that be, Captain? You have not gone and made a bloody fool of yourself over a wench again?"

"I have *not*," Diego said firmly, giving Scurvy a dagger look that would have easily silenced a less stubborn man. But the first mate was unwilling to accept the strange wench so easily.

"What have you been doing to our good captain here, missy?" he demanded of her. "Making the best of his generosity, I'll have no doubt!"

"*Scurvy*," Diego ground out in a stern voice that would brook no further argument. "One more harsh word out of your infernal mouth to her ears and I swear I will punish you for it."

The first mate gave him a look of incredulity, but he did not open his mouth directly to Cat again. Instead, the three of them sat around the rickety kitchen table, while Diego splashed drinks into plastic tumblers for the two men and Scurvy related his amazing tale.

"Aye, I was pulled under by the waves," the older man said, reverently sipping his rum, "but I finally surfaced again, far out to sea. Many days there I was, I know not how long, but there were a few bits of flotsam to hang on to. Dying of thirst and hunger is what I was, I tell you. But just when my grip, so to speak, Captain, began to slip, you will never guess what happened."

"Enlighten us," Diego suggested, dashing another finger of rum into Scurvy's glass.

"A ship appeared out of nowhere," the old man whispered. "A fine ship, the likes of which I have never seen before. At first, I imagine it must be a dream, see, or the onset of sailor's delirium. But nay, I am pulled on board and delivered to the ship's doctor. Can you imagine, Captain, a ship so large they carry their very own doctor? Well, 'pinch me,' I say to the strange man, for very oddly dressed the beggar is, 'pinch me,' I say, 'for I must be dreaming.' It wasn't long before I discovered why every person on board appeared so strange and why the ship itself appeared to be no less than a miracle. For it must have been heaven's magic that brought us to this time, Captain. There is no other way to explain it."

"Aye," Diego agreed, glancing over the top of

Scurvy's head toward Catalina. "I still believe it is that, myself. A miracle."

"Well, it's coy I was with this information, Captain, not wanting to reveal myself for a complete lunatic, which is clearly what all twelve hundred aboard would make of me were I to say precisely *when* I'd come from."

"Twelve hundred, mate?" Diego asked, clearly intrigued. "That must have been quite a ship."

"Never have you seen her equal," Scurvy insisted. "A *cruise ship*, she was. Built, if you can believe it, for nothing but sport and pleasure. In fact, I have been motoring around the islands on her for near a month now in the most amazingly luxurious style. Free food galore—nightly feasts fit for a king. Aye, and the women on board—*wealthy* women, if you please, wearing nothing more than great gobs of jewelry and tiny scraps of *bathing suits*. Women with all of their teeth intact, Captain. It was paradise on earth. I thought I had died and gone to heaven for sure."

"A month of all this easy living and joy-seeking?" Diego asked with a perceptive grin. "Have you gone soft on me, old man?"

"Nay," he responded, "and more's the pity. The captain of this great vessel gave me succor at first, imagining myself to be an unfortunate victim of amnesia, possibly caused by a bump to me head from the bow of his speeding ship."

Diego's eyebrows lifted in cool, amused inquiry.

"I cannot imagine where he got such an unlikely idea."

Scurvy grinned appreciatively. "I'll lay wager you can, Captain."

"Well then, go on. Why were you finally set on shore again?"

"Kicked cruelly from the very land of the lotus-eaters, I was," he groaned sorrowfully. "Or in this case, the ship of them. That captain said I had been given ample time to recover from me injuries and me cruising days had come to an end. I believe the fact that I had run up a great deal of shipboard credit and could not remember the location of me banking account also had something to do with it."

"No doubt," Diego answered dryly.

"Many fine memories have I taken away from this sea adventure," Scurvy added wistfully. "And interesting new ideas as well. Simply consider this for a moment, Captain. That ship I sailed on was but one of many cruising the seas at this very moment. One of many loaded with wealth and goods galore. Sitting ducks they are, with no cannon on board at all. Can you imagine it, Captain? An entire fleet of cruise ships, completely indefensible, right there for the taking!"

Diego seemed to digest this information for a moment. He took a sip of his rum, seeming to consider the angles of Mr. Scurvy's wild, piratical plan.

Cat's heart grew cold with fear. He wasn't even *thinking* about going back to that way of life, was he? The whole idea of plundering cruise ships was too crazy to even contemplate. But there was something glittering in the depths of those blue eyes that Cat had never seen before. A hunger. A gleam. A thirst for adventure.

She knew him too well to misread the momentary yearning that flashed across his handsome face. He *did* miss the old roving life. He missed what he had agreed to give up for her.

He shook his head slowly as the look left his eyes. "The plan has much to recommend it," he admitted, out of consideration for his first mate or true belief, Cat wasn't sure. "But it is likely not as easy as it appears," he cautioned. "The modern *technology* of warships is quite formidable. I am afraid it would be wiser to choose another way of life more suited to this day and age, mate. Privateering is quite out of style in this century."

Mr. Scurvy appeared thunderstruck. "Give up swashbuckling, Captain? Have you gone mad?" He glanced from Diego to Catalina and back again. "It is the wench who has done this to you, man, is it not? Bewitched you with her womanly ways, I'll make no doubt!"

"That's enough, Scurvy," Diego said, rising from the table. "We will discuss it at greater length later. It's growing late. There is a cot in the attic for you to sleep on. Not especially comfortable, but it will suffice until we figure out what is to be done."

Thus summarily dismissed, Mr. Scurvy moved to leave, but not before shooting still another suspicious glance Cat's way. He lifted the bottle of rum from the table, turned, and tottered unevenly up the stairs.

Diego resumed his spot at the table and downed the last of his drink. "Catalina," he said. "I am sorry for his behavior toward you. He is an old man, set in his ways. He fears you mean to change me."

"It is not his behavior that worries me," Cat admitted softly. "It's yours."

TEN

"My behavior, Catalina?" Diego asked, his frown a mirror of confusion. "I do not understand you. What is it I have done to cause you concern?"

Cat let out a long sigh, rubbing her forehead, wondering how to explain to him exactly what her concerns were. It was late. It had been a long day, and both of them were weary with all that had happened. Maybe that was what was wrong with her. She was simply exhausted, both emotionally and physically.

But she was upset as well as tired, and she didn't want to spend her wedding night in a state of worry. She wanted to clear the air between them, smooth over the doubts that Mr. Scurvy's sudden appearance had created in her mind.

"I guess I'm just surprised," she said, "that you would even consider Mr. Scurvy's plan. Diego, it's crazy!"

"Of course it is, Catalina. I would not consider such a thing. Did I not promise you earlier that I was through with plundering for good?"

She hesitated. "Well, yes, but for a minute there you were thinking about it, weren't you?"

He put a hand to his chin, scratching at the day's growth of dark stubble. "I will admit the plan had a certain reckless, impossible appeal to it. But it was the challenge of it that intrigued me, *cara*, nothing more."

"And a desire not to disappoint your old friend?" she added.

"Aye," he agreed, "that, too. Mr. Scurvy will require some time adjusting to the idea that I am a pirate no longer."

"Diego," she said, "I'm not sure you've had enough time adjusting to it yourself."

His frown deepened as he seemed to consider her statement at length. "I have taken the first step," he finally responded, "by starting a new life with you."

Cat shook her head slowly, feeling her stomach grow queasy. "Is that why you married me?" she said. "As a consolation prize for the past you've lost? Is that why you failed to mention to Mr. Scurvy that you *are* a married man, now?"

"*Cara*," he said, "you are talking crazy."

"Am I?" she asked him, firing up in anger. An anger that was sparked by sudden fear. Couldn't he see how afraid she was? "Do you know how you introduced me to him? As Ms. Steadwell, *not* Mrs. Swift."

"A mere slip of the tongue, lass."

"A *Freudian* slip. Don't you see? You didn't tell him, because deep down inside you really don't *want* to be married. You want to be free again to sail off with Scurvy to Lord knows where doing heaven only knows what!"

Cat knew she was completely losing it by this time, but she really couldn't stop herself. She wanted Diego to stop her, instead. She wanted him to take her in his arms and kiss her fears away and reassure her that everything would be all right.

She wanted him to tell her that he loved her.

He didn't.

He planted his empty glass on the table with a heavy thud, folded his arms across his chest and stared at her as if she'd entirely lost her mind. "Is that all the faith you have in me, Catalina? No more than a peso's worth? Do you imagine I would go back so easily on the promise I made to you?"

"No!" she exclaimed angrily. "The great Captain Swift is clearly far too proud for that! I expect you would keep your promise to me no matter how much you wanted to break it!"

"Indeed?" he asked, his voice lethal, simmering with barely controlled anger. "Then you give me far too much credit. Believe me, sweet, if I had it in my mind to sail off with Mr. Scurvy on the morrow, nothing would stop me! Nay, not even you."

Cat was close to tears by now. The only thing keeping her from breaking down was her pride. Diego wasn't the only one who had more than enough of that commodity, and she refused to let him see her in such a state.

But what was he saying? That she was right? That he did want to go off and leave her?

She didn't think she could bear it if he did. But it was better to find out now, wasn't it? Better to give him his walking papers sooner rather than later. If he wanted his freedom so badly, he could *have* it!

She stood from the table, keeping her chin high as she stared down at him. God, but it hurt just to look at him. It hurt to speak. "Believe me, Captain Swift, I wouldn't dream of trying to stop you. In fact, I'll make it easy for you. So easy you can leave anytime you like. I'll set you free of the vows we made. Free of the marriage."

She tore the woven ring from her hand, dropping it onto the table in front of him, waiting for him to say something, anything.

He didn't say a word.

There was no "please, *cara*," no "of course I wish to stay married to you, sweet." There was only bitter, painfully bleak silence.

Cat's worst fears were confirmed. Diego did want his freedom back. He wanted to be rid of her.

His face was drawn, his eyes blazing with unspoken anger. Why didn't he say something? What had happened to all those incredible communication skills he'd demonstrated on the beach? This man in front of her was nothing like that kind and caring lover who'd taken her to paradise with him this very afternoon. This person was cold and silent, a man she barely recognized.

A pirate who had stolen her heart and was about to make off with it.

Catalina wasn't prepared to give it up without a good fight. Any reaction would be preferable to his awful silence.

"Coward," she breathed, intending to get a rise out of him.

It worked. He stood from the table, backing away from her, his nostrils flaring, his black hair flying. "Is this what you think of me, woman? That I am not only a liar and a man who would break his word, but a coward as well? It is no wonder you wish to return my ring to me. Indeed, you are far better off without me if that is how you feel."

"It *is*," she insisted, feeling her throat tighten and the tears beginning to burn terribly at the back of her eyes. "Only a coward would give his woman up without a fight!"

"Nay," he said fiercely. "Only a coward would sink low enough to fight a woman. I cannot argue with you, Catalina, any more than I can slay dragons that do not exist."

"Dragons?"

"The ones you have created. You knew what I was, who I was when we agreed to marry, and nothing has changed since then. But it is not a real husband that you want. It is a paper document, much like the deed to this house, that you can lock away in a drawer to prove what does and does not belong to you. Had we been married in my time, *you* would have belonged to me. But if there is one thing I have learned from my time-traveling experiences, it is that *nothing*, in truth, belongs to us. You will never be able to lock me away in that drawer. You will never be one-hundred-percent sure of me. You are still seeking proof of my love, but there is none left to give."

He reached for the small ring that was still resting on the table, a beacon of love in the middle of a very bad dream. He slipped it into his pocket.

Cat's chest tightened as she struggled to swallow back a sob. She stared at Diego, feeling stunned, as though he'd hit her. He meant it, she realized, feeling desperate.

He was hers no longer. He had never been hers.

He was a pirate once more.

"I am setting you free as well, Catalina," he added, his voice tight, terrible, raw with emotion. A muscle clenched in his jaw. "You do not belong to me."

Cat turned away from him, her body shaking from the blow he'd just dealt her. She had thought she was strong enough to battle with Diego. She'd been a fool.

What had happened between them in the last five minutes? What had happened to the man she had been in love with enough to marry? The coldness in his tone ripped at her heart, tore her up inside. Had she been mistaken in her judgment of him?

It wasn't possible. She'd lived with him for a

month, laughed, shared, *loved* with him. How could she have been so wrong?

The tears finally came, harsh and stinging, dropping onto her eyelashes and cheeks in spite of her efforts to hold them back. They tasted of salt, reminding her sharply of the ocean, of the taste in Diego's mouth when he'd kissed her. It was too much for Cat to take.

She ran from the room without looking back.

The sound of Catalina's feet rushing up the wooden staircase to her bedroom was as brutal to Diego's ears as a barrage of bullets from a firing squad. Had his old enemies been there to witness it, the greedy Mayan-robbing barons of the merchant fleets, they would have been right pleased to know how deep and wrenching was his pain. In five minutes, Catalina had accomplished what they had not managed to achieve in fifteen years. His punishment.

Aye, she had killed him quite effectively. She had returned his ring and in so doing ended any hope he might have had for a life of love. A life of peace, free of fighting and running. Free of piracy.

It was a life he had likely never deserved in the first place. But the angels had answered a prayer he had never been aware of making, and had sent him forward across the centuries to meet his match. Catalina Steadwell, the woman he had fallen in love with, the woman who for a few short hours had been his wife. She had been taken from him as suddenly as fate had seen fit to throw them together.

She had lost faith in him, lost trust. She had made

him lose faith in himself. A bloody fool he had been to ever believe it could work in the first place.

Their marriage had been doomed from the moment it was made. No two people had ever been so mismatched. A scoundrel and a saint. What hope had they of making their loving last?

Very little it seemed, since their promises had survived for less than a day. Their passion was not enough to ward off the outside world. Had they stayed on that islet forever, it might have worked. But such isolation from time and society was not possible.

Their love was not possible.

She had accused him of being proud. Aye, he was proud enough to be wounded to the quick by her poor opinion of him. She had imagined he would go back on the promise he made, and meant, from the bottom of his heart. But it was his very heart she had called into question.

A dark and shriveled blackguard's soul she believed him to possess. A fine man she imagined her new husband to be—the sort who would walk out on her at the first hint of temptation to come along in the doubtful form of Mr. Scurvy. Aye, he was as fond of his first mate as any good son would be of a man who had treated him as such.

But to give up his new life in the hopes of having the old one back?

He harbored no such hopes. It had not been such a fine, romantic way of life, after all. To be stuck in the company of scores of restless men for months on end, with no wenches, no washrooms, and no hope of obtaining either, was not half as adventuresome as the Errol Flynn movies suggested.

Nay, a sense of ocean-faring freedom was all well and good, but many was the time he had wished for this voyage or the other to come to an end. Never more so than when his loyal crew was in the throes of seasickness, and half of them hanging their heads over the side before their bodies adjusted to the motion again. Such grand, adventurous sights and smells as that he could well do without.

But just when he was beginning to get his feet planted firmly on the ground in this new era, Catalina tells him that he is welcome to leave, that he is wishing for his freedom.

Well, he did *not* wish for it. But perhaps she was right about one thing. Perhaps the both of them would be far better off on their own.

She certainly would. And if he did not share the same sentiment for himself, more was the pity. Time away from her for a while was what he needed now. Time to consider his future.

"Ms. Steadwell?" a female voice asked. "The doctor will see you now."

"Oh!" Cat was jolted out of her daydream by the appearance of an efficient, uniform-clad nurse who ushered her from the semicrowded waiting room directly to Dr. Wenckly's office.

"Your test results are in," the woman said in a

firm voice, pointing Cat toward a chair and placing a marked manila file folder on the top of the doctor's vacant desk.

Cat caught herself leaning forward in her chair slightly and staring at the ominous object with a mixture of anticipation and dread. As if her entire future depended on whatever was in that harmless-looking little folder.

Which it did.

Yes, that was her file, all right. She could see her name typed clearly on the bright red tab. She had a sudden urge to reach across the doctor's desk and rip it open, but from the forbidding way the nurse was eyeing her, she decided it might not be such a good idea.

She sat back in her chair, instead, looking down at her hands, pretending to study her manicure, making a supreme effort to appear perfectly serene. There was something about that disapproving nurse—maybe it was the crisp, authoritative uniform, maybe it was simply the look in her eye—but she was starting to remind Cat of the sisters back at school.

Oh, Lord, she could only imagine what the nuns would think if they could see her now. Unmarried, alone, and waiting for the results of her pregnancy test.

Yes, it was a red-letter day for strict nuns everywhere.

A scarlet-letter day. The good Catholic girl who had strayed from the fold only two and a half weeks ago was about to have her sins weighed. She was about to find out, one way or the other, whether heaven's judgment had gone for or against.

She looked up again and was stunned to find herself staring into a pair of startling blue eyes. Her heart did a wild flip before she realized they belonged to Dr. Wenckly and not to another man. No, the good doctor didn't look a thing like Diego. He was short and slightly stocky, brown-haired and impeccably dressed. A successful man of science.

He cleared his throat, opened the file folder and carefully examined the documents within. Cat held her breath, glancing silently around the room, up at the ceiling, anywhere but at the face of the man who would read her sentence. The nurse had disappeared. At least her humiliation would be a private one when the verdict was finally read. Because she knew what the reliable Wenckly was going to tell her before the words were even out of his mouth.

Dear Lord, *she knew*.

"Positive," he said, making no attempt to ease her into the information slowly. "It seems your instincts were correct, even though conception was relatively recent. You are definitely pregnant, Ms. Steadwell."

"I see."

Cat blinked, wondering when the thunderbolt would be arriving from above to strike her down. Or maybe that *was* the thunderbolt the doctor had just delivered. Oddly, it wasn't half as horrible as she had imagined.

There was no wailing and weeping for her lost innocence, no nuns trying to beat down the consulting room door and drag her off in an attempt to hide her shame. There was only the calm voice of Dr. Wenckly, dispensing his advice on prenatal care.

He didn't even bat an eye at her obvious state of singlehood! She wore no ring, and the information was all right there in her chart, anyway. But it was the nineties now, not the sixties, and unwed mothers were apparently no big deal in this day and age.

At least, not to Dr. Wenckly. He finished delivering the maternity spiel to her, filed the test results back in her chart and stood to shake her hand.

"Congratulations," he said, and seemed to mean it. "The nurse has some pamphlets to give you. Please follow them as thoroughly as you can, and I'll see you back here in six weeks."

Cat nodded and mumbled something she hoped was appropriate in return, duly collected her pamphlets, and drove herself home in a daze.

She was pregnant. She was going to have Diego's child.

His illegitimate child.

But instead of feeling sick and depressed and completely disappointed in herself for the terrible sin she'd supposedly committed, she felt . . . happy. Yes, surprisingly excited. There was a baby growing inside her. A new life.

How could she bring herself to start weeping over a miracle like that?

Of course, the conditions the child would be born into were less than ideal. Having two loving parents around to raise a baby would naturally be better than just one. But she had no choice now except to make the best of it.

Diego was not coming back.

Cat realized that now. He had been gone from the house for two and a half weeks without a single word. It had seemed like an eternity to her since she'd woken up the morning after their fight, puffy-eyed, weak from a restless night of weeping, and found him gone.

Vanished without a trace, along with Mr. Scurvy.

She had given him his freedom, and he had taken her up on it. He had been right about one thing. Her faith in him hadn't been strong enough. Her fears that he might rove again had come to pass.

She had *forced* them to come to pass. She had goaded him into leaving, into giving up on them before they'd barely had a chance to get started. Was that what he'd been trying to tell her that night?

She had wanted an iron-clad guarantee that he would *never* leave her the way her parents had. A guarantee in the form of a marriage license that he belonged to her. But he had said there were no guarantees, that nothing really belonged to a person permanently.

She supposed it was a lesson Diego had learned by losing everything in the hurricane. Even the house that had been his seaside refuge had wound up in her hands, as it would belong to someone else long after she was gone.

Time was fleeting. Possessions were ephemeral.

Love was the only thing of lasting value.

If that was the lesson he'd tried to pass on to her, Cat was sorry she'd learned it too late. He was gone. For good.

If it hadn't been for the major improvements he'd made in the house, the empty bottle of rum she'd found in the attic, and the small pink seashell nestled protectively under her pillow, she might have thought the whole interlude with him was no more than a dream.

A sweet, sensuous dream she wished she'd never awakened from.

But the thought of a baby growing deep within her had a way of bringing her back to reality, fast. She had someone else to think of now. Someone to look out for, to protect. Someone to love.

She wanted this baby, she realized. If the decision had been left entirely up to her, she still wasn't sure whether or not she would have chosen to become pregnant. It seemed somewhat selfish to deny a child a lifelong relationship with its father.

Being born a child of love, she was terrified that the same stigma might apply to her own son or daughter. But she knew her offspring would be raised in a different world. Dr. Wenckly's blasé reaction to her single state had shown her that.

Whatever came their way in this world, she knew that they would handle it together.

Diego was no longer hers. Maybe he never had been. But this child definitely would be.

Their child. His seed had found its way inside her, taken root, blossomed into the closest thing to a miracle she could imagine.

The only part of him she had left.

ELEVEN

Cat awoke early the next morning to the sound of a distant siren blaring somewhere outside her bedroom window. Instinctively, she put her hand down and cradled it against her stomach. It was funny how pregnancy changed your perspective. About everything. Her first thought was not for her own safety, but for her baby's.

Any doubts she'd once had about this neighborhood were suddenly amplified by the idea of raising a child in it. Was it a desirable environment for a baby? Probably. But if it turned out to be otherwise, she would have few reservations about moving.

Funny, too, that the house didn't seem as important to her as it once had. It was still beautiful in its own ancient way, still historically worth saving, but without Diego, it seemed empty. More a house than a home.

As for a future without him—she would just have

to handle that one day at a time. *No guarantees*, she reminded herself. Yes, that was the lesson she'd learned from a certain buccaneer who had made his living by taking risks.

Life itself was a risk. It was time to get on with hers.

She headed for the bathroom, promising herself a long, hot shower. The jets of water streaming down on her skin were wonderfully warm, lapping at her body as beautifully as the ocean waves had stirred around her that day at the tiny island. Thanks to Diego's sensual thoroughness with the protective suntan lotion, her face had been the only part of her to get slightly sunburned that afternoon, and the last traces of pink nose and peeling skin finally disappeared with a thorough scrubbing, revealing a fresh, new woman underneath.

A woman Cat barely recognized when she toweled off and studied herself in the mirror. She wasn't sure if it was the pregnancy or the natural face peel, but she was *glowing*. All of her greatest fears had come to pass, but miraculously, she was still there.

She had survived them.

And if she could manage to go on without the man she loved, she figured she could make it through almost anything. The heartbreak of losing him was still there, a constant ache, but in time, the pain would probably diminish, or maybe she'd just grow numb. Either way, she was learning to adjust to it.

She had faced her fears head-on and discovered she was even bigger than they were. She was no longer that scared little girl who had always felt so out of place at school. No longer the troubled young woman who still carried the scars of abandonment. But she was still a child of love.

She had learned to love herself.

She had learned to depend on herself—the hardest lesson of all. Wasn't that the first step in getting over her heartbreak?

She slipped into a short, feminine dress of vibrant summer green and blew her hair dry, letting it fall to her shoulders in shimmering auburn waves, a departure from her usual practical, pinned-back style. The sunshine had lightened it by several shades and for the first time since Diego's departure, Cat's heart felt a little lighter as well.

True freedom, she realized, was more a state of mind than anything. You didn't have to go sailing off somewhere on a wild search for adventure to find a challenge. There were plenty to be faced and fought and conquered right here. Yes, she had managed to slay a few dragons all by herself.

Was that why Diego had walked out on her? So she could discover her own inner strength? Or was she still creating false hopes in her mind, still harboring the thought that he might return to her one day?

Return to *them*.

She made her way down to the kitchen, determined to read over every one of Wenckly's pamphlets in great detail, then scramble herself up a nutritious breakfast, but a strange jiggling sound at the front door stopped her dead in her tracks.

Someone was trying to break into the house! The knob was turning back and forth, but the new lock, thank goodness, was holding securely. She'd had it installed since Diego's departure as an added security measure, along with a super-duper dead bolt. She was *tired* of people trying to barge in on her at all hours. Wasn't what had happened to her the last time someone had managed to break in bad enough?

She heard a male voice swearing in frustration on the other side. A familiar voice. Her breath caught, but she stood rooted to the spot, unable to even *hope* that she knew who it belonged to.

Diego.

"What the devil?" she heard him say, followed by what sounded like a kick to the outside of her nice new knob. His old key clearly did not work, and at this rate it would only be minutes before he decided to bash the whole door in again.

Cat took a deep breath and stepped forward to open it. But instead of Diego standing expectantly on the other side, he came flying in, shoulders first, and wound up dive-bombing onto the foyer floor with a sickening thud.

"Oomph!"

Apparently he'd been trying to break it down with that amazingly well-muscled body of his the very second she'd decided to let him in. Poor man. She'd bet a peso or two that all those muscles were going to be black and blue before too long.

"Blast it all to hell and back!" he exclaimed, groaning. "Are you trying to kill me, Catalina?"

Cat folded her arms across her chest in cool self-composure and stared at him calmly. "Don't you ever knock?"

"Not when I want to get into my own house, I don't!" he complained, sitting up with a wince, starting to dust himself off.

"Your house?" she asked doubtfully. "I don't know about that, bub . . ."

"Now, sweet," he said, raising himself up off the floor and starting to come toward her. "Do not let us start that again. Are you not pleased to see me?"

"No," she lied, keeping her arms folded defensively and slowly backing away from him. "I am not."

He stopped then, raking a wave of black hair away from his eyes and planting his hands on his hips in a stance of sheer male frustration. "Blast and damnation, *cara*, but you are one stubborn woman."

"Thank you. But that's Ms. Steadwell to the likes of you, Captain Swift."

He folded his arms across his chest, eyeing her narrowly. "Still angry at me, are you, lass?"

"Furious," Cat agreed sweetly.

He stroked a hand across his chin, apparently trying to gauge what his next move should be. "Perhaps a bit of good news would settle you down, sweet."

"Indeed? Have you decided to move? To Siberia, I hope?"

"Nay," he said, grinning appreciatively. "An ornery wench such as you should not be so lucky as that. My good news has to do with a certain birth certificate. Lass, it has finally arrived."

Cat stared at him suspiciously. "How do you know that?" she demanded.

He strolled to the couch, settled himself back against the cushions and folded his arms casually behind his head. "Simple," he said proudly, reaching into his shirt pocket and producing the document in question. "I have pilfered it from your mailbox."

"I might have known," she answered dryly.

But in spite of her valiant effort at nonchalance, Cat felt her heart skip a beat at the news. With his new identity in hand, Diego would be free to, to— *No.* She couldn't even bring herself to wish for something as wonderful as that.

"Do you know what this means, Catalina?" he said, finishing the thought that she had been too cautious to even contemplate. "We can be truly married at last. Legally this time."

Cat didn't respond immediately to this miraculous piece of news. She couldn't. She was too stunned, too confused. Did he still want to marry her? Would she even be willing to forgive him for the way he'd walked out on her?

He pulled her down beside him on the couch, taking her by the shoulders and giving them an urgent little shake. "Is this not what you have wished for all along? Please say you will give me a second chance, Catalina."

The blue of his eyes was burning into her, searing her senses, trying to see straight into her soul. She wasn't the only one who was hurting, she realized. Diego had done some suffering of his own these past few weeks if the emotion in his voice was anything to go by. And the word *please*. She couldn't remember an occasion when the proud pirate Swift had used that humble expression before.

"You walked out on me," she reminded him rationally. "You said you wanted your freedom back."

"Nay," he corrected her. "It was you who tried to tell me what I wanted. I was angry at you for it. Angry that you did not believe in the vows we had made to each other. I am not a man who is used to having my word doubted."

"I have no problem believing that," she told him, attempting a wry smile.

"I wanted to teach you a lesson," he admitted, "and I am right sorry, my love, that I went about it in such a reckless way. It seems Douglas Smith still has much to learn himself."

"I learned a lesson, all right," Cat said softly, "but Diego, you hurt me. I had no idea where you were. I thought you were never coming back. In fact, what I really learned is that I would still be okay if you didn't come back."

He swore quietly, shaking his dark, handsome head in self-disgust. "I wanted to prove to you that you were stronger than you realized, lass. But when you put it like that, I would prefer to hear you say that you could not survive another moment without me and that the lack of my suave, swashbuckling company has sent you into a deep and dismal decline.

Indeed, I have behaved like a bloody fool by reminding you that having a pirate around your house serves no necessary purpose."

She smiled at that, her heart softening in spite of her wellspring of strength. "Would it make you feel any better if I had a case of the fits, or maybe fainted right here on the spot?"

"Nay, sweet," he said regretfully, "I know you far too well for that. I have never succeeded in making you swoon, in spite of my concerted efforts to do so. The only thing that would help at this moment would be for you to agree to marry me."

"I've already agreed to that once," she told him stubbornly. "It didn't work."

"It is too late, then?" he asked, his tan face growing pale. "In fact, you love me no longer. You still believe that I am a scoundrel and a coward."

"Diego," she whispered, "I'm sorry I called you that. I'm sorry for everything. I was—afraid."

"No more than I am now, *cara*," he said gruffly, "of losing you for good." He tilted her chin up. "Have I lost you, lass?"

Catalina found herself starting to drown again in the deep, dreamy blue of his eyes. They darkened with desire, growing irresistibly sincere and sexy. He had missed her, she realized. A lot. And she had to accept her own responsibility for the argument they'd had.

She met his gaze solemnly. After all, it wasn't just her own welfare that was at stake any longer. "Have you really come home to stay this time?"

"Aye," he swore soundly.

"And I can count on you not to go traipsing off again at the first sign of an argument?"

"Nay," he agreed. "Next time we have a lovers' quarrel, I promise to stay and fight. If only to be around to make up with you later," he added, a speculative gleam in his eye.

He took her in his arms then and buried his face in her hair. Cat was touched by the depth of emotion she felt in his massively muscled body as it shuddered with relief. So much feeling, she thought, and all of it for her.

Diego did love her. Thank God. She should never have doubted it.

"You will take my name, then, Catalina, and be my wife?" he asked, pulling back to look at her. "Swear it, sweet."

"I will," she promised him, her throat constricting with happiness and relief. "I swear."

He took her face between his hands, cradling it gently. "I did not give you the reassurance you needed that night, Catalina. I did not tell you I loved you. More than my freedom. More than anything. I will say it now, as often as you need to hear it. *Te amo, cara.* I love you. I will keep saying it until you truly believe me."

Cat thought her heart would melt at the sound of Diego's wondrous words. "I do believe you," she told him. "I believe that's why you came back to me. But I don't think I'll ever get tired of hearing you say it. Diego," she added, "I love you too."

"Do you suppose you can learn to love Douglas as well?" he asked, grinning.

"I believe I could even grow fond of you as an Eleazar," she admitted, smiling back.

He squeezed her hands tight, and Cat decided the time had finally come to break her biggest news. "I have something else I need to say to you now, as well."

"Indeed?" he asked, looking intently into her eyes. "I am listening."

She took a deep breath. "I'm—expecting."

The dark eyebrows lifted in uncomprehending confusion. "Expecting? Expecting what, lass?" he asked glancing toward the door as if a package was about to be delivered at any moment.

"Oh, it's a bundle all right," she exclaimed, laughing. "But not the kind you're thinking."

"Nay? What sort of bundle will be arriving, then, Catalina?"

She leaned forward, whispering the answer softly in his ear. "A baby."

The dark eyebrows drew together. "Someone is bringing a baby to our door, *cara*?"

"No!" Cat exclaimed, taking his large hand in hers and placing it over her belly. "We are going to *have* a baby. And we will be bringing it through that door, about eight months from now."

Diego was momentarily speechless. He stared down at her stomach, awestruck. "A little one? Can it be true?"

"It can," Cat assured him. "It is."

He stood up from the couch, pacing the room as if the news was simply too big to handle sitting down. "But this is wonderful!" he exclaimed, throwing his arms wide and continuing to strut up and down the length of the floor, apparently very proud of his accomplishment. "Can you imagine it, Catalina? I will teach him to fence and to sail, I will teach him—"

"Him?" Cat cut in, grinning. "How do you know it's going to be a 'him'?"

He stopped, seemed to consider this for a moment, then continued his swaggering, pleased-as-punch walk. "Then I shall teach *her* how to sail and fence. Only, think of it, Catalina, the child will be part of both of us—the miraculous result of our love."

"A love child," she said, still smiling.

"Aye," Diego agreed, pulling her up beside him and into his arms for a long, heartfelt hug. "The best kind of child to have."

Cat allowed herself to relax in Diego's powerful, protective arms.

"I promise you, *cara*," he said, still holding her hard, "our babe will have the legal documents that you were lacking. We will be married long before it is born." He drew back to study her. "I cannot wait to see you in your wedding gown."

"Going to make a legal woman of me, are you?" she teased. "Well, I'll have to admit that the name Catalina Swift does have a certain appealing ring to it."

"Speaking of *rings*, sweet," he said, "I have brought you one back from my trip that will serve far better than the pitiful substitute I gave you before." Reaching deep into the pocket of his blue jeans, he withdrew a small, sparkling object and slipped it onto her hand before she had time to speak.

"An engagement ring," he explained, bringing her fingers to his lips and kissing them, a roguish gleam in his eye. "I hope you are pleased with it."

Pleased? Cat stared at the enormous emerald and fabulous antique filigree mounting in a state of disbelieving shock. It couldn't be real. It was too *big* to be real. Too *beautiful*.

Diego merely laughed at her gasp of soft astonishment. "The green suits you so well, sweet. Of course, if you wish to choose some other style or color—"

"No!" she exclaimed. "This is—perfect. But, Diego, where did you get it? I mean, I don't *mind* if it's a simulated stone or something like that—"

"It is not," he assured her proudly. "It is quite genuine."

"Quite *valuable*, you mean," Cat said, her stomach beginning to churn with worry. "This emerald is the most magnificent green I've ever seen. And the size of it. It has to be at least five carats!"

"Ten," he corrected her.

"Ten?" Cat squeaked, visions of imminent bankruptcy floating wildly through her mind. They could not possibly afford such a spectacular treasure. She didn't know how or where he'd purchased it, but it would simply have to go back.

Oh dear. If he *had* purchased it at all. Her mind screened back to the powerboat incident and the episode with Crazy Al. She hoped to heaven he hadn't been browsing in the local jewelry store and imagined he could test-drive an engagement ring!

"Diego," she said cautiously, not wanting to hurt his feelings, "you didn't—"

She was saved temporarily by a knock at the door. Diego answered it and Mr. Scurvy walked in, grinning from ear to ear.

"Top of the morning to you, lass," he said cordially to Catalina. "Captain," he added, bowing in a gentlemanly fashion to Diego, then tossing him a shiny new set of keys. "The yacht is moored down at the dock all right and tight," he said. "All ready for you when you are ready for her again."

"The—yacht?" Cat asked in growing astonishment.

"Aye," Scurvy told her, plopping himself down on their living room couch and stretching his short bowlegs out onto the coffee table. "And a right lovely one she is. Handles smooth, too. No chance of being seasick on a ship as streamlined as that one. Cuts through the waves like a sharp steel blade, leaving nary a wake behind her."

Cat narrowed her eyes at him, wondering exactly what this pair had been up to for the past two weeks. Mr. Scurvy's sudden turnaround in behavior toward her was odd enough, but she really began to grow alarmed when she noticed what the former first mate was wearing. A cream silk summer suit that had designer written all over it, not one, but *two* brand-new gold watches, one for each wrist, and a pair of leather high-top, high-style tennis shoes with the name of some sports superstar emblazoned gaudily across the sides. He looked like an expensive closet just fell on him.

She really had no problem with his questionable sense of fashion, but there was one thing she needed to know.

Where had the two of them gotten all the money?

"Okay, Diego," she said, turning back toward him and folding her arms across her chest. "Spill it. Where did you guys go, anyway? Fort Knox?"

"Eh, Catalina?"

"Don't you dare eh, Catalina, me! You know exactly what I'm talking about. Ten-carat emerald rings. Designer wardrobes. Yachts! You always wanted to make me faint? Well, believe it, Swift, I'm about to!"

"Settle down, sweet," he said, a worried look on his face. "You'll upset the babe."

"The baby's really going to get upset when it has to visit his daddy in jail!" she told him, only half-joking.

Her mind was working feverishly in an effort to figure out where all this loot had come from. Meanwhile, Scurvy and Diego were congratulating each other gleefully over the news of her pregnancy.

"A wee pirate in the making, eh, Captain?"

Scurvy suggested with a wink. "Always knew you had it in you, mate!" he exclaimed, slapping Diego on the back. "Indeed, I'd say this calls for a bit of rum." He headed for the kitchen cabinet, prepared to help himself to a friendly toast.

"Stop!" Catalina cried. "There is no more rum, Mr. Scurvy. You drank it all during your last visit, remember? Now, will somebody *please* tell me where you have been all this time."

"*Cara*," Diego said, putting a soothing arm around her. "We will tell you all you wish to know. Only sit down here beside me on the couch and put your feet up. Good, lass. Now, the answer to your question is quite simple. First, you will be pleased to know that we have both retired from our questionable profession of piracy."

"Aye," Scurvy agreed, grinning hugely. "What is the point in plundering when I am already rich beyond my wildest dreams?"

"Rich?" Cat repeated, looking expectantly at Diego. "And just where did this sudden windfall come from?"

An image of an unguarded cruise ship and a pair of rakish, raffish buccaneers sneaking stealthily over the side came horribly to mind. She shuddered. "Diego, you didn't . . ."

"I promise you, Catalina, we swashbuckled no one. At least we have not done so for nearly two hundred years. We were on a business trip these past weeks. At least, I was."

"Business?" Cat asked skeptically.

"Aye," Scurvy agreed, "and a dreadful, boring, business it was, spending time with *him*. I assure you, Catalina, there is nothing more pitiful than a lovesick pirate, which is exactly what I have had to put up with. Many was the time I wished to throw him overboard, so sunk in dismay he was. Never have I seen him in such a state. Marry him lass, and quick. Aye, you are welcome to him!"

"Thank you," Cat told him. "I think."

"If you are quite finished now?" Diego asked Scurvy, lifting his eyebrow at him in cool inquiry.

"Of course, Captain. Go on."

"My business," Diego said bluntly, "was raising the interest of investors in a new company I wish to start. Mr. Scurvy was good enough to introduce me to several of the well-off people he had met on his cruising adventure. One widow in particular was amazingly pleased to renew her acquaintance with him. In short, Mr. Scurvy has become engaged to a very wealthy woman."

"Wealthy, would you say, Captain?" Scurvy asked in conjecture. "I might venture to describe her as the widow of Croesus himself."

"Either way," Diego said, grinning at Cat. "Mr. Scurvy is about to become leg-shackled. As soon as *his* new birth certificate arrives, that is. We have also paid a visit to the library, you see."

"Aye," Scurvy said, shaking Cat's hand gratefully. "I understand it is you I have to thank for that clever idea, Catalina."

"Think nothing of it," Cat responded, still a bit

confused. She was incredibly relieved to hear that they hadn't pilfered the cruise-ship industry after all. But Scurvy—married? She hoped the woman he'd picked knew what she was getting herself into!

"Now, Cat," Diego said, "I know what you're worrying about, lass, but I assure you that everything is aboveboard. This widow is more than a match for our Mr. Scurvy."

"True, Captain," Scurvy agreed. "Already cracking the whip over me poor old head, she is. Expects me to give up rum completely, can you imagine it? Says it's bad for me health! It's fond of her I am, but how, I ask you, am I supposed to achieve a state of wedded bliss without a nip every now and then?"

Diego grinned. "That, Mr. Scurvy, is an image which stretches the limits of credibility. We wish you good fortune in achieving such a state, however," he added, glancing intently at Catalina. "I believe it has much to recommend it."

"For the present," the older man told them with a twinkle, "a bit of rum is exactly what I'm needing to celebrate. Sorry, Captain, but as there is none in the house, I must take me leave of you to go in search of a dab or two before I am cut off from the mother's milk completely." He bowed graciously to Catalina again, sent Diego a mock salute, and headed out the door.

Cat settled back in the crook of Diego's arm, trying to take it all in. "But if it's Scurvy that's going to be marrying money," she said, "where did the emer-

ald come from? And is it his yacht," she added, "or
yours?"

"The ring is all yours," he told her, "a wedding
gift from Scurvy and his soon-to-be bride."

Cat shook her head slowly. "It's too valuable,
Diego. We can't accept it."

"You would hurt their feelings most sorely if you
returned it," he explained gently, "but I will leave
that decision up to you. But you should know the
gesture was meant only to please you and, in so doing, to please me as well. It seems they are truly
grateful for your idea, which made it possible for
them to marry."

Cat glanced up at him in surprise. "You mean she
knows who he is and *when* he came from?"

"Aye," Diego said, "and I believe it is the challenge of reforming Mr. Scurvy that interests her the
most."

"Really?" Cat asked, laughing. "I can't wait to
meet her."

"Indeed," Diego told her, "I believe you two will
find much to talk about. Now, as for the yacht, Catalina, that does not belong either to my old first mate
or to myself. It is the property of Crazy Al, in fact."

"Crazy Al? He actually let you borrow another
one of his boats?"

"Better than that," he informed her. "Al has
agreed to back my new business venture. Since the
funding has come through for your restoration project, you will be able to hire a better handyman than
myself. And I have it in mind, sweet, to do something

useful with my new life. I plan to enter the ship-racing contest called the *Admiral's Cup*. With a sleek, new sailing ship that my company will one day design."

"Yacht racing?" she asked. "Diego, that sounds perfect for you. Where did you ever get the idea?"

"Television," he told her, grinning. "*The Adventure Channel.*"

She laughed up at him, her senses going soft just from looking at him. Her heart was so full at the moment, she wasn't sure how to handle such a flood of happiness. It was all going to work out, somehow. She and Diego were really going to find their happily-ever-after, after all.

She tipped her head back then as Diego bent to kiss her. Life with him would always be an adventure, she realized, a warm and exciting series of risks and explorations, of wins and, sometimes, losses. But it was a voyage they would share together.

He deepened the kiss, cradling her in his arms, plumbing her mouth sweetly as his heat and strength flowed into her. Cat was melting again, marveling at the need she felt for him, reveling in the urgent response he showed for her. Her pirate was going to need a great deal of attention to keep him out of trouble and happy at home. And Cat was just beginning to dream up ways to make sure that he got plenty of it.

"Just remember," she told him, whispering warmly against his lips, "that your days may be filled with all sorts of new sailing adventures, but your nights belong to me."

"Mmmm, *cara*," he said hoarsely, "that is a promise I can willingly make."

Cat laid a hand on her stomach, a tender reminder of the baby now growing inside her and the passion that had brought it into being. The past and the present would combine in their child to create the exciting promise of the future.

As for the immediate present—she could hardly wait to share that lovely antique bed upstairs with Diego. On this night she would show him the very best thing about the marvelous, modern world of the twentieth century. Not a new invention by any means, but an age-old miracle that still had the ability to transcend time.

The eternal power of love.

TWELVE

The two couples strolled across the deck of the *Windward*, arm in arm as the evening stars came out. The constellations glittered against the ocean's smooth surface like a shower of small diamonds scattered by a summer rain. Catalina Smith glanced up at her handsome husband and smiled.

"Douglas," she said, "I don't think I've ever seen so many stars in my life. Are nights at sea always so beautiful?"

"Nay, lass," he told her, "many are the nights that are *not* so calm. And the heavens are clearly visible because we are so far from civilization and those infernal electric lights that normally obscure the sight. But the view is an unusually lovely one," he added, glancing down at her.

They stopped momentarily by the railing of the ship as he took her in his arms and bent to kiss her.

"Enough of all that gazing and kissing, you two!"

one. Only three names in all," he explained, "and two of them girls'. I was obliged to take the only one remaining, which, as you know, ended in Prescott."

"But your first name," she prompted.

Mr. Prescott bit his lower lip, reluctant to reveal it.

Cat glanced up at Douglas and saw his blue eyes gleaming brilliantly with unspoken mirth. "How bad could it be?" she asked him.

"It is *worse*," he said solemnly, "than Eleazar."

"Aye," Mr. Prescott admitted sorrowfully. "It is rather awful, indeed. It is *Knud*."

"Knud?" Cat repeated, incredulous. "I'm not even sure I know how to spell it."

"Rotten luck," Mr. Prescott said, "is it not?"

Douglas threw his head back and roared with laughter.

Uncertain of her own ability to keep a straight face, Cat led her husband away, promising to meet up with the Prescotts later. They were back at their cabin before she finally broke down, laughing until her sides hurt.

"Poor Mr. Scurvy," she said, finally regaining some sense of composure.

"Mr. Prescott," Douglas assured her, "is far from poor. Do not feel sorry for him, sweet. He is a lucky man, overall, although not nearly as fortunate as I."

"Thank you," Cat said, her voice going soft as she read the familiar gleam in her husband's eyes. "Now, we only have two and a half hours remaining before the midnight buffet," she reminded him. "Would you like to take a tour of the bridge?"

"No," Douglas told her, pulling her down beside him on the king-size bed. "I would not."

"Some evening shuffleboard then?" she suggested, smiling. "Or maybe you'd prefer to attend a lecture about the island we'll be visiting tomorrow. I understand they even have a legend about a wicked pirate who once sailed these waters. Bluebeard."

"Bluebeard!" Douglas exclaimed scornfully. "A mere mama's boy. Now, were the legend about a swashbuckler named Diego Swift . . ."

"Oh?" Cat asked him. "Then this Swift fellow was, in fact, quite a scoundrel?"

"Incorrigible," he told her. "A regular rogue. Even kept love slaves in the attic of his house."

"Quite a man with the women, was he?"

"Aye. Until one woman came along who was quite good with him. Indeed, it is a fascinating story with the most *satisfying* ending imaginable. Lie back against the pillows, lass, and I will tell you all about it . . ."

THE EDITORS' CORNER

Everybody has a classic story that has endured in their heart through the years. There's always that one story that makes you think *What if . . . ?* This month we present four new LOVESWEPTs, each based on a treasured tale of the past, with their own little twists of fate. It is said that differences keep people apart, but we've found the opposite to be true. Differences make life interesting, adding zest and spice to our lives. We hope you'll enjoy exploring those differences in opinion, station, and attitude that ensure a happy ending for our LOVESWEPT characters this month.

In Pat Van Wie's **ROUGH AROUND THE EDGES,** LOVESWEPT #870, Kristen Helton is about to meet her match in one doozy of a hero, Alex Jamison. Alex grew up on the streets of Miami and now he's devoted his life to keeping the local community center open. But when Kristen insists on joining his fight to keep kids out of trouble, Alex has to accept that he may have been wrong about the gorgeous young doctor. The tensions run high after Alex decides to sacrifice himself to raise money for the center. Kristen discovers his secret and comes to realize that maybe their worlds aren't so different after all. In the true tradition of Robin Hood, Pat Van Wie delights as she shows us how we must persevere against all odds.

Maureen Caudill is giving Jason Cooper his comeuppance in **NEVER SAY GOOD-BYE**, LOVESWEPT #871. When last seen, Jason was playing the part of die-hard bachelor scoffing at his sister and best friend's domestic bliss in **DADDY CANDIDATE**, LOVESWEPT #797. Years later, C. J. Stone's magazine names Jason the Sexiest Businessman in California. Now Jason is desperate to get C.J. off his back and believes that a nerdy facade will make her change her mind about him. C.J. and Jason seem to disagree about everything. Even watching *It's a Wonderful Life* causes a clash of beliefs between them. But the one thing they can't argue about is their growing attraction to each other—it's undeniable. With humor and grace, Maureen Caudill plots a collision course for these mismatched lovers.

Stephanie Bancroft retells the story of Aladdin in **YOUR WISH IS MY COMMAND**, LOVE-SWEPT #872. "I shall grant you three of your heart's desires" is the last thing Ladden Sanderson expects to hear after an earthquake reduces his antiques store to a shambles. Jasmine Crowne doesn't understand why now, after three years of friendship, she suddenly longs to feel Ladden's arms around her. And no one can explain the strange man who keeps muttering something about wishes—or the antique carpet Ladden is reserving for Jasmine that keeps popping up in the weirdest places. Can a benevolent genie help this quiet diamond in the rough win over the woman he's always loved? Stephanie Bancroft charms readers as she weaves a delectable romance liberally spiced with marvelous miracles and fantasy.

Five years ago Liam Bartlett was saved from a San Salustiano prison with the help of young freedom fighter Marisala Bolivar. Now Mara is all grown up and both are about to learn **FREEDOM'S PRICE**, LOVESWEPT #873, by Suzanne Brockmann. When Mara's uncle sends her to Boston to get an education and, unbeknownst to her, learn to be a proper lady, he asks his friend Liam to take care of her, to be her guardian. Liam finds it harder and harder to see Mara as the young girl she once was, but his promise to her uncle stands in his way. Mara has loved Liam forever, and she does her best to get him to see her as the woman she has become. Suzanne Brockmann seals the fate of two lovers as they learn to battle the past and look to the future.

Happy reading!

With warmest wishes,

Susann Brailey

Joy Abella

Susann Brailey
Senior Editor

Joy Abella
Administrative Editor

P.S. Watch for these Bantam women's fiction titles coming in January! Hailed as "an accomplished story-teller" by the *Los Angeles Daily News*, nationally best-selling author Jane Feather concludes her charm bracelet trilogy with **THE EMERALD SWAN**. An exquisite emerald charm sets in motion a tale of suspense, laughter, and love, and brings together twin girls separated on a night of terror. Newcomer Shana Abé delivers **A ROSE IN WINTER**. In the year 1280, a time of dark turbulence, Solange is forced to scorn her greatest love in order to protect him, an act that leaves her imprisoned in the terrifying reaches of hell until Damon becomes her unwitting rescuer. From *New York Times* bestselling author Iris Johansen comes a new hardcover novel of suspense, **AND THEN YOU DIE. . . .** Photojournalist Bess Grady witnesses a nightmarish experiment conducted by international conspirators. With the help of a mysterious agent, Bess escapes their clutches, vowing to do whatever it takes to stop them from succeeding in their deadly plan. And immediately following this page, preview the Bantam women's fiction titles on sale in December!

For current information on Bantam's women's fiction, visit our new Web site, *Isn't It Romantic*, at the following address:

http://www.bdd.com/romance

closet and checking the small wooden chair she'd jammed beneath the doorknob in the middle of the night.

The chair was still in place. She released the breath she'd been holding and sat up. The empty room was already bright with mid-morning sun, the adobe walls golden and cheery. The air was hot. Her T-shirt stuck to her back, but maybe the sweat came from nightmares that never quite went away. She'd once liked mornings. They were difficult for her now, but not as difficult as night, when she would lie there and try to force her eyes to give up their vigilant search of shadows in favor of sleep.

You made it, she told herself. *You actually made it.*

For the last two years she'd been running, clutching her four-year-old daughter's hand and trying to convince Samantha that everything would be all right. She'd picked up aliases like decorative accessories and new addresses like spare parts. But she'd never really escaped. Late at night, she would sit at the edge of her daughter's bed, stroking Samantha's golden hair, and stare at the closet with fatalistic eyes.

She knew just what kind of monsters hid in the closet. She had seen the crime scene photos of what they could do. Three weeks ago, her personal monster had broken out of a maximum security prison by beating two guards to death in under sixty seconds.

Tess had called Lieutenant Lance Difford. He'd called Vince. The wheels were set in motion. Tess Williams had hidden Samantha safely away, then she had traveled as far as she could travel. Then she had traveled some more.

First, she'd taken the train, and the train had taken her through New England fields of waving grass and industrial sectors of twisted metal. Then she'd caught a plane, flying over everything as if that would help her forget and covering so many miles she left behind even fall and returned to summer.

Landing in Phoenix was like arriving in a moon crater: everything was red, dusty, and bordered by distant blue mountains. She'd never seen palms; here roads were lined with them. She'd never seen cactus; here they covered the land like an encroaching army.

The bus had only moved her farther into alien terrain. The red hills had disappeared, the sun had gained fury. Signs for cities had been replaced by signs reading STATE PRISON IN AREA. DO NOT STOP FOR HITCHHIKERS.

The reds and browns had seeped away until the bus rolled through sun-baked amber and bleached-out greens. The mountains no longer followed like kindly grandfathers. In this strange, harsh land of southern Arizona, even the hills were tormented, flayed alive methodically by mining trucks and bull-dozers.

It was the kind of land where you really did expect to turn and see the OK Corral. The kind of land where lizards were beautiful and coyotes cute. The kind of land where the hothouse rose died and the prickly cactus lived.

It was perfect.

Tess climbed out of bed. She moved slowly. Her right leg was stiff and achy, the jagged scar twitching with ghost pains. Her left wrist throbbed, ringed by a harsh circle of purple bruises. She could tell it wasn't anything serious—her father had taught her a lot about broken bones. As things went in her life these days, a bruised wrist was the least of her concerns.

She turned her attention to the bed.

She made it without thinking, tucking the corners

tightly and smoothing the covers with military precision.

I want to be able to bounce a quarter off that bed, Theresa. Youth is no excuse for sloppiness. You must always seek to improve.

She caught herself folding back the edge of the sheet over the light blanket and dug her fingertips into her palms. In a deliberate motion, she ripped off the blanket and dumped it on the floor.

"I will not make the bed this morning," she stated to the empty room. "I choose not to make the bed."

She wouldn't clean anymore either, or wash dishes or scrub floors. She remembered too well the scent of ammonia as she rubbed down the windows, the doorknobs, the banisters. She'd found the pungent odor friendly, a deep-clean sort of scent.

This is my house, and not only does it look clean, but it smells clean.

Later, Lieutenant Difford had explained to her how ammonia was one of the few substances that rid surfaces of fingerprints.

Now she couldn't smell ammonia without feeling ill.

Her gaze was drawn back to the bed, the rumpled sheets, the covers tossed and wilted on the floor. For a moment, the impulse, the sheer *need* to make that bed—and make it right because she had to seek to improve herself, you should always seek to improve—nearly overwhelmed her. Sweat beaded her upper lip. She fisted her hands to keep them from picking up the blankets.

"Don't give in. He messed with your mind, Tess, but that's done now. You belong to yourself and you are tough. You won, dammit. You *won*."

The words didn't soothe her. She crossed to the

bureau to retrieve her gun from her purse. Only at the last minute did she remember that the .22 had fallen on the patio.

J.T. Dillon had it now.

She froze. She had to have her gun. She ate with her gun, slept with her gun, walked with her gun. She couldn't be weaponless. *Defenseless, vulnerable, weak.*

Oh God. Her breathing accelerated, her stomach plummeted, and her head began to spin. She walked the edge of the anxiety attack, feeling the shakes and knowing that she either found solid footing now or lunged into the abyss.

Breathe, Tess, breathe. But the friendly desert air kept flirting with her lungs. She bent down and forcefully caught a gulp by her knees, squeezing her eyes shut.

"Can I walk you home?"

She was startled. "You mean me?" She hugged her school books more tightly against her Mt. Greylock High sweater. She couldn't believe the police officer was addressing her. She was not the sort of girl handsome young men addressed.

"No," he teased lightly. "I'm talking to the grass." He pushed himself away from the tree, his smile unfurling to reveal two charming dimples. All the girls in her class talked of those dimples, dreamed of those dimples. "You're Theresa Matthews, right?"

She nodded stupidly. She should move. She knew she should move. She was already running late for the store and her father did not tolerate tardiness.

She remained standing there, staring at this young man's handsome face. He looked so strong. A man of the law. A man of integrity? For one moment she found herself thinking, If I told you everything, would you save me? Would somebody please save me?

"*Well, Theresa Matthews, I'm Officer Beckett. Jim Beckett.*"

"*I know.*" Her gaze fell to the grass. "*Everyone knows who you are.*"

"*May I walk you home, Theresa Matthews? Would you allow me the privilege?*"

She remained uncertain, too overwhelmed to speak. Her father would kill her. Only promiscuous young women, evil women, enticed men to walk them home. But she didn't want to send Jim Beckett away. She didn't know what to do.

He leaned over and winked at her. His blue eyes were so clear, so calm. So steady.

"*Come on, Theresa, I'm a cop. If you can't trust me, who can you trust?*"

"I won," she muttered by her knees. "Dammit, I won!"

But she wanted to cry. She'd won, but the victory remained hollow, the price too high. He'd done things to her that never should have been done. He'd taken things from her that she couldn't afford to lose. Even now, he was still in her head.

Someday soon, he would kill her. He'd promised to cut out her still-beating heart, and Jim always did what he said.

She forced her head up. She took a deep breath. She pressed her fists against her thighs. "Fight, Tess. It's all you have left."

She pushed away from the dresser and moved to her suitcase, politely brought to her room by Freddie. She'd made it here, step one of her plan. Next, she had to get J.T. to agree to train her. Dimly, she remembered mentioning her daughter to him. That had been a mistake. Never tell them more than you have to, never tell the truth if a lie will suffice.

Maybe J.T. wouldn't remember. He hadn't seemed too sober. Vincent should've warned her about his drinking.

She didn't know much about J.T. Vince had said J.T. was the kind of man who could do anything he wanted to, but who didn't seem to want to do much. He'd been raised in a wealthy, well-connected family in Virginia, attended West Point, but then left for reasons unknown and joined the Marines. Then he'd left the Marines and struck out solo, rapidly earning a reputation for a fearlessness bordering on insanity. As a mercenary, he'd drifted toward doing the impossible and been indifferent to anything less. He hated politics, loved women. He was fanatical about fulfilling his word and noncommittal about everything else.

Five years ago, he'd up and left the mercenary business without explanation. Like the prodigal son, he'd returned to Virginia and in a sudden flurry of unfathomable activity, he'd married, adopted a child, and settled down in the suburbs as if all along he'd really been a shoe salesman. Later, a sixteen-year-old with a new Camaro and even newer license had killed J.T.'s wife and son in a head-on collision.

And J.T. had disappeared in Arizona.

She hadn't expected him to be drinking. She hadn't expected him to still appear so strong. She'd pictured him as being older, maybe soft and overripe around the middle, a man who'd once been in his prime but now was melting around the edges. Instead, he'd smelled of tequila. His body had been toned and hard. He'd moved fast, pinning her without any effort. He had black hair, covering his head, his arms, his chest.

Jim had had no hair, not on his head, not on his body. He'd been completely hairless, smooth as marble. Like a swimmer, she'd thought, and only later understood the full depth of her naiveté. Jim's touch had always been cold and dry, as if he was too perfect for such things as sweat. The first time she'd heard him urinate, she'd felt a vague sense of surprise; he gave the impression of being above such basic biological functions.

Jim had been perfect. Mannequin perfect. If only she'd held that thought longer.

She'd stick with J.T. Dillon. He'd once saved orphans. He'd been married and had a child. He'd destroyed things for money. He sounded skilled, he appeared dangerous.

For her purposes, he would do.

And if helping her cost J.T. Dillon too much?

She already knew the answer, she'd spent years coming to terms with it.

Sometimes, she did wish she was sixteen again. She'd been a normal girl, once. She'd dreamed of a white knight who would rescue her. Someone who would never hit her. Someone who would hold her close and tell her she was finally safe.

Now, she remembered the feel of her finger tightening around the trigger. The pull of the trigger, the jerk of the trigger, the roar of the gun and the ringing in her ears.

The acrid smell of gunpowder and the hoarse sound of Jim's cry. The thud of his body falling down. The raw scent of fresh blood pooling on her carpet.

She remembered these things.

And she knew she could do anything.

From award-winning author Patricia Potter comes a spectacular novel set in the wild Scottish Highlands, where a daring beauty and a fearless lord defy treachery and danger to find their heart's destiny . . .

STARCATCHER

by Patricia Potter

Marsali Gunn had been betrothed to Patrick Sutherland when she was just a girl, yet even then she knew the handsome warrior would have no rival in her heart or her dreams. But when Patrick returns from distant battlefields, a bitter feud has shattered the alliance between clans, and Marsali prepares to wed another chieftain. Boldly, Patrick steals what is rightfully his, damning the consequences. And Marsali is forced to make a choice: between loyalty to her people or a still-burning love that could plunge her and Patrick into the center of a deadly war . . .

"Patricia Potter has a special gift for giving an audience a first-class romantic story line."
—*Affaire de Coeur*

"One of the romance genre's finest talents."
—*Romantic Times*

He had dreamed of her. It was so much more than she'd ever expected. Her legs trembled as his tongue touched her lips, then slipped inside her mouth. A wave of new sensations rushed through her. Yet she did nothing to discourage the intimate way he explored her. Instead, she found herself responding to his every touch.

Somehow, with what was left of her wits, she realized she was clinging to him, as if her life were forfeit. She heard the small, throaty sounds she was making. She felt his entire body shaking, and she felt the hard, vital evidence of his manhood pressed against her. She had heard servants talk; she knew where this was leading. And she wanted it, wanted to move even closer to him, to join her body intimately with his.

But she could not build her own happiness on the blood of others, especially not the blood of her kin and the kin of the man she loved.

She had to return to Abernie. She had to go through with the wedding. . . .

Tearing herself from Patrick's embrace, Marsali let out a pained, hopeless cry. Surprised, Patrick let her go, his arms dropping to his sides. His breathing was ragged as his eyes questioned her.

"I canna," she said brokenly.

"We were pledged," he replied, his voice hoarse. "You are mine, Marsali."

The note of possessiveness in his voice, even given the feelings he aroused in her, stunned her. The flat, almost emotionless tone was so authoritative, so . . . certain. He'd become a stranger again, one who made decisions without consulting her.

"Our betrothal was broken," she said quietly, "cried off by both families."

"Not by me," he said.

She studied him obliquely. "My father and Edward . . . they will go after your family," she said.

"They will *try*." Coldness underlined his voice.

"Your father killed my aunt," she said desperately.

"Nay, my father is as puzzled by her disappearance as any man, and, despite his faults, he does not lie."

"Not even with death as a consequence?"

"Not even then."

Lifting her chin a notch, Marsali continued. "He accused my aunt of adultery."

"He says there was proof," Patrick replied.

His eyes glittered with the hardness of stone, and she glimpsed what his enemies must have seen of Patrick Sutherland. The thought of him at war with her father and brother made her shiver.

Dear Mother in heaven. The wedding should have started by now. Everyone would be looking for the bride. When would they begin to suspect the Sutherlands?

"I have to return to Abernie," she whispered.

"Jeanie said she would not help us if she wasn't sure you didna want the wedding," Patrick said flatly. "Was she wrong, lass? Do you want to wed Sinclair?"

"Aye," Marsali said defiantly, even though she was certain the lie must be plain on her face.

"Because of your sister?" Patrick guessed.

"Because you and I can never be."

He studied her for a moment, then, slowly, the tension left his face. He lifted his hand to trail a finger along her cheek. "You have become a beautiful woman," he said quietly. "But then, I always knew you would."

Her resolve melted under the words, under the intensity of his gaze, under the force of his demand for the truth. She leaned into his touch, craving it.

His hands were strong, she thought, from years of wielding a sword. But she could well destroy him, as well as both of their families, if she did not return.

"I *agreed* to the marriage with Edward," she said as firmly as she could. "I gave him my troth."

His hand trailed downward over her shoulder, her arm, until he took her hand in his. He squeezed her fingers, saying, "You had already given it to me with your words and, a minute ago, you gave it to me with your body. Your heart is mine, Marsali."

"And *your* heart?" she asked.

A muscle flexed in his throat, but he said nothing, and she wondered for a moment whether he had come for her out of affection—or simply because she was a belonging he wasn't ready to forfeit.

She pulled away and turned to gaze at the rocks, the hills, anything but the face made even more attractive to her by the character the years had given it. "Where would we go?"

"To Brinaire," he said flatly.

"And Cecilia?"

"Aye, she will come with us. You will both be safe there."

"Your father? He agrees?"

He hesitated long enough that she knew the answer.

"He will have to," he said. "Or we will go to France. I have friends there."

She turned and looked at him again. "And then our clans will fight one another. Many will die or starve because of us. Can you live with that?"

His mouth twisted. "They seem destined to fight now in any event."

"But there has been naught but a few minor raids," she said. "If I were to go with you, my father would not be satisfied with anything but blood. His pride—"

"Damn his pride!" Patrick burst out. "I canna

stand aside and see you marry Sinclair. The man is a coward. And his wife's death was more than a little odd."

When she only stared at him, saying nothing, he sighed heavily and shoved his fingers through his thick, black hair. Her gaze followed the gesture, falling on the scar on his wrist that he'd gotten saving her ferret's life so many years ago. Reaching out, she took Patrick's hand in hers, her fingers touching the rough, white mark from the hawk's talons. Its jagged length ran from the first knuckle of his fourth finger down his forearm to four inches past his wrist.

"Will you make an oath to me, Patrick Sutherland?" she asked, lifting her gaze to meet his.

"Aye," he said, nodding slowly. "Anything but return you to Sinclair."

"Send my sister away. Send her someplace safe. I know only my father's friends."

His gaze bore into hers. "I do know someone. Rufus's family. I was wounded, and they cared for me. There are five sisters, as well as Rufus and an older brother and his wife. It is as fine a family as I've ever known—and as generous a one. They live in an old keep in the Lowlands and socialize very little, though they bear a fine name. Their clan is very loyal to them."

"Will you see her safely there? Do you swear? No matter what happens between you and me?" She heard the desperation in her voice and saw, by the fierce glitter in his eyes, that he'd heard it, too.

"I swear it, lass," he said.

"Thank you." Marsali closed her eyes briefly.

She didn't resist when he took her in his arms again, pulling her gently toward him. She leaned against him, listening to the beating of his heart, the fine strong rhythm of it, and savoring the warmth of his body.

For a long minute, she huddled within his embrace, trying not to think of Abernie Castle, trying not to imagine the worry everyone—everyone but Jeanie—must be feeling by now. Shortly, when a search of the castle didn't turn up either her or Cecilia, panic would seize them. The two daughters of the keep gone without a trace.

She had to return. Still, she would not be returning the same person as she was when she left. Fear had turned into hope, if not happiness. Patrick had given her the means to refuse the marriage to Edward Sinclair. As long as she knew Cecilia was safe, no one would be able to force the words from her mouth. And by refusing marriage with Sinclair, she would break the alliance that would have crushed Patrick's family. Her father could not attack the Sutherlands on his own. Perhaps a war could be prevented, after all.

She would make her father believe that no Sutherland was involved in her sister's disappearance. Only herself. He would be furious. But he could do little.

Her heart would never be whole again. She could already feel it breaking, shattering into tiny shards of pain. But she would have the comfort of knowing she had prevented bloodshed.

She only wished that, one day, her father—and brother—might understand what she had given up.

On sale in January:

*AND THEN
YOU DIE . . .*
by Iris Johansen

*THE EMERALD
SWAN*
by Jane Feather

*A ROSE
IN WINTER*
by Shana Abé

DON'T MISS ANY OF THESE EXTRAORDINARY BANTAM NOVELS

On Sale in December

THE PERFECT HUSBAND
by LISA GARDNER

A terrifying paperback debut about a woman who
put her husband behind bars, became his next target
when he broke out, and had to learn to fight back
to save her own life—this un-put-down-able
novel is a non-stop thrill ride!

____ 57680-1 $6.50/$8.99 in Canada

STARCATCHER
by PATRICIA POTTER

A powerful story in which war and
feuding families conspire to keep apart two lovers
who have been betrothed for twelve years.
But, like Romeo and Juliet, they are determined
to honor a love meant to be.

____ 57507-4 $5.99/$7.99 in Canada

DON'T MISS THESE FABULOUS BANTAM WOMEN'S FICTION TITLES

On Sale in January

AND THEN YOU DIE...

by IRIS JOHANSEN

the New York Times *bestselling author of* THE UGLY DUCKLING

When an American photojournalist stumbles into a sinister plot designed to spread terror and destruction, she will do anything—risk everything—to save her family and untold thousands of innocent lives.

_____ 10616-3 $22.95/$29.95

THE EMERALD SWAN

by the incomparable JANE FEATHER,
nationally bestselling author of VICE *and* VANITY

A major bestselling force whom the *Los Angeles Daily News* calls "an accomplished storyteller," Jane Feather pens the much anticipated third book in her "Charm Bracelet" trilogy: the mesmerizing tale of twin girls who grow up as strangers—and the dark and magnetic Earl who holds the key to their destinies.

_____ 57525-2 $5.99/$7.99

A ROSE IN WINTER

from the exciting new voice of SHANA ABÉ

Brimming with passion and intrigue, enchantment and alchemy, England is brought to life in its most turbulent time, as two lovers risk political exile and certain death to keep their love in bloom.

_____ 57787-5 $5.50/$7.50

Ask for these books at your local bookstore or use this page to order.

Please send me the books I have checked above. I am enclosing $_____ (add $2.50 to cover postage and handling). Send check or money order, no cash or C.O.D.'s, please.

Name _____

Address _____

City/State/Zip _____

Send order to: Bantam Books, Dept. FN159, 2451 S. Wolf Rd., Des Plaines, IL 60018.
Allow four to six weeks for delivery.
Prices and availability subject to change without notice.   FN 158 1/98